ALSO BY JOSEPH CILLO JR.

Merry Friggin' Christmas: An Edgy Christmas Comedy

When the Wood Is Dry: An Edgy Catholic Thriller

Elektra Voltare: Blessed with Awful

Elektra Voltare: Eve of the Memes

Elektra Voltare: Instrument of God

BLIND PROPHET COMIC BOOKS

Episode 1: A Prophet Is Born

Episode 2: Spiritual Warfare

Episode 3: The Prophet Goes to Washington

Episode 4: The Great Demon of Pride

Part I (Includes Episodes 1 thru 4)

Get Blind Prophet, Episode 1: A Prophet Is Born for **FREE!**

For details, please visit: www.edgycatholic.com

THE GHOST OF HALLOWEEN PAST

AND OTHER CATHOLIC TALES FROM THE EDGE...

JOSEPH CILLO JR

Published by Infornuity Publishing LLC, Flemington, NJ

For more information go to: www.edgycatholic.com :

*The Ghost of Halloween Past
and Other Catholic Tales from the Edge*
Copyright © 2024 Joseph Cillo Jr.

All rights reserved. No part of this book may be used or reproduced in any manner whatsoever without written permission except in the case of brief quotations embodied in critical articles or reviews.

This book is a work of fiction. Names, characters, businesses, organizations, places, events and incidents either are the product of the author's imagination or are used fictitiously. Any resemblance to actual persons, living or dead, events, or locales is entirely coincidental.

Illustrations in this book were created in Adobe Photoshop, using the generative fill feature.

Book design by Joseph Cillo Jr.
Cover design by Joseph Cillo Jr
EBook ISBN: 978-1-942590-49-1
Paperback ISBN: 978-1-942590-48-4
Hardcover ISBN: 978-1-942590-47-7

First Printing : 2024

For all the little ones...

GHOST OF HALLOWEEN PAST

AND OTHER CATHOLIC TALES FROM THE EDGE

SOME COMMENTS FROM THE AUTHOR

PREFACE

THE GREAT CATHOLIC WRITER, Flannery O'Connor once wrote:

> The novelist with Christian concerns will find in modern life distortions which are repugnant to him, and his problem will be to make these appear as distortions to an audience which is used to seeing them as natural; and he may be forced to take ever more violent means to get his vision across to this hostile audience. When you can assume that your audience holds the same beliefs you do, you can relax a little and use more normal ways of talking about it; when you have to assume that it does not, then you have to make your vision apparent by shock—to the hard of hearing you shout, and for the almost blind you draw large and startling figures.

That bit of wisdom was originally published in 1957. If Catholic writers required shouting and large and startling figures to get their point across in 1957, what might be required in 2024? Perhaps a hard slap in the face?

Having descended a bit into despair after witnessing the man recognized as pope of the Catholic Church participating in pagan ceremonies in the Vatican Gardens and leading prayers to a pagan idol in St. Peter's Basilica, I struggled to complete the novels I had started. In fact, I had to alter the world in my Edgy Catholic Dystopian Series to feature the "Catholic Church of All Religions" rather than the Holy Roman Catholic Church under persecution from secular authorities.

With the confusing events of the times, it became harder to throw myself completely into large projects. I discovered the weekly contests on Reedsy.com and decided to create some short fiction based on their prompts in my Edgy Catholic style. While I did not anticipate winning these contests, I paid the five-dollar entry fee just to make sure that someone read my stories.

As expected, the stories did not win any prizes, but in putting them together as a collection, I believe, I have created a sum that is greater than its parts. My style is more direct than Flannery's, however. Many people miss the Catholicism in her work. Unfortunately, the time for subtlety is over and even large and startling figures have lost their impact. And so, with apologies to any theologians who find deficiencies in my representations of the faith in these confusing times, brace yourself for some good, hard, Catholic slaps in the face.

THE GHOST OF HALLOWEEN PAST

AND OTHER CATHOLIC TALES FROM THE EDGE...

A CATHOLIC SLAP IN THE FACE...

TRIGGER WARNINGS: Any reader who needs a trigger warning for anything should not read this book. The stories deal with edgy material, and while there is no foul language nor nudity, any number of other things might trigger a sensitive reader.

CONTENTS

"Therefore thus saith the Lord: Behold I devise an evil against this family: from which you shall not withdraw your necks, and you shall not walk haughtily, for this is a very evil time. In that day a parable shall be taken against you..."–Micah 2:3-4 (Douay-Rheims Bible)

THE GHOST OF HALLOWEEN PAST

AND OTHER CATHOLIC TALES FROM THE EDGE

THE GHOST OF HALLOWEEN PAST

AND OTHER CATHOLIC TALES FROM *THE EDGE*...

MARTA DREAMS OF A MYSTERIOUS GIRL WITH FLOWERS IN HER HAIR

THE GHOST OF HALLOWEEN PAST

Reedsy.com prompt: *Write a story about someone who is haunted. Whether by a ghost or something else is up to you.*

MARTA PREPARED A LUNCH for her daughter Kristin and wrote on the brown paper bag the name, "Emily." Closing her eyes tightly, she gripped the counter for a moment, then crumpled the bag and threw it in the trash.

She had no daughter named Emily. She had never had a daughter named Emily and would never name a daughter Emily. She hated the name Emily ever since she had caught her old ex-friend Emily Tyson sucking face with her old ex-boyfriend, Clyde whatever-his-name-was. That was long ago. There were so many names. Why would she ever choose Emily as a name for a child? But that was the child's name in her dream, in that nightmare world where she mothered a child named Emily, cared for her, and made her lunch.

She rolled her eyes and took out another bag and began writing an "E," again. She stopped herself and sloppily transformed it into a "K," and completed the name Kristin. She sighed. This girl from her dreams haunted her.

And it was October, a time for haunting. The leaves had turned and begun to fall, swirling in their haphazard way, in the cool breezes of autumn. *Autumn?* That would be a nice name for a daughter. Why had she not dreamt of a daughter named Autumn?

But it was always Emily, never any other name in her dreams. And it galled her, because she loved this girl, Emily. The girl was cute and vivacious, pigtailed, and always in the same print dress covered with those little blue flowers, the same little blue flowers in her hair, five petals like the points of a star around a yellow center. Kristin was moody. Her moods ranged from sullen to sassy. And she rarely wore dresses and despised flowers. Why would anyone despise flowers? But that was Kristin. Maybe it was just a phase. Kristin was at that age where children had phases. But did she love this dream girl more than her own daughter? The thought horrified her.

Marta glanced up at Kristin, who was finishing her breakfast cereal at the kitchen table. "Finish up, Kristin. You'll have to hurry to make the bus."

Kristin glanced up at the ceiling as she dropped her spoon into her bowl and rose from her chair. She flung her bookbag over her shoulder and picked up her bag lunch. She glanced at it, pursed her lips and squinted. "So, who's Emily?"

"What? Emily?" Marta stammered.

Kristin held up the bag and pointed to the name. "Yeah, Emily?"

Marta sighed. She took out another brown bag. "Please, Kristin, write your own name on the bag."

Kristin took the pen and scrawled on the bag. She held it up for her mother. "Is that better?"

Marta examined the bag. "Now, that's not funny. Please write your own name on the bag, not Emily."

Kristin crinkled her brow. "I wrote Kristin. See?"

She traced over the letters as she spoke, "K R I S T I N, Kristin."

Marta blinked and looked over the bag, again. "I'm sorry, Kristin. I have not been sleeping well. I could swear it said Emily."

Kristin rolled her eyes, transferred her lunch into the new bag and put it into her book bag. "You're so weird."

Kristin scurried off to catch the bus.

Marta glanced down at the bag. How could she have written Emily twice? She specifically recalled changing the E to a K and writing Kristin, but the evidence was indisputable. And how could she have seen Emily in what Kristin had written? Emily, Emily, Emily! Why Emily?

She shook her head. There was no sense to make of it. The Emily she had known, what had happened to her? That was back in high school. Had she married Clyde whatever-his-name-was? Had he murdered her, so now, the ghost of Emily sought revenge for her letting her have Clyde all to herself, only to find he was a murderer? That was just crazy. Besides, the girl in her dream was about Kristin's age, maybe a little younger. She wasn't old enough for the drama of high school and wouldn't be thinking about kissing a boy.

Maybe it was some other trauma that caused her troubled dreams? She had had some bad times with men before she was married. She forced herself not to think about it. They were very bad times. They were the times she shut out whenever she went to that supermarket next to *that place*. But there was no Emily in that story. And no Clyde what's-his-name. And no murderer. But there was a violent crime as bad as murder. Or almost as bad. Committed by a nameless man with only a vague description recorded in a police report filed with the cold cases.

Marta shuddered and forced herself to think of something else. That reality was worse than her nightmare. Or was it?

"Emily, those flowers are so pretty!"

Emily giggled. "Thank you, Mommy. Do you know what they are called?"

"Why, no. I don't. I think I used to know, but I can't seem to remember now. Whatever they're called, they suit you so well. They bring out the blue in your eyes."

"Mommy..."

Marta stopped the memory of her dream before it turned into the nightmare. She would not let her conscious mind relive that part of her dream.

She would have to go past *that place* again today. Buying candy for the kids, after all it was Halloween. She didn't like Halloween. It brought back the memories of the bad times. It was a time when bad things happened. But the children expected candy. And the children made Halloween bearable. She grabbed her keys and went to her SUV. She started the car and turned on the radio. Nothing but static, and then one station tuned in. It was that religious station. She shook her head. She hadn't much use for religion. After all, nameless men lurked in church parking lots and bad things happened. She closed her eyes and thought of something else, anything else. Even Emily. That sweet, happy child of her dreams. But not the end of that dream. Never the end.

"I kept having this dream," the voice on the radio said. *Dream?* "This dream that I was looking for my baby, and I couldn't find her. There were all these other babies, but none of them were mine. I would wake up crying, saying, 'where's my baby!'"

Marta turned the radio off. She had never had that dream. She had her baby. Kristin. She couldn't bear to think about losing her child. She had never lost a child.

She drove to the supermarket. They really should not put those places next to supermarkets. They should not be where people have to see them. She focused on the road as she passed *that place*. She would use the entrance furthest from it, park as far from it as she could. Why did she glance over? But she did. And she saw them, protesting. What business was it of theirs?

She recalled walking past them with her escort. He would make sure she got into *that place* safely. "Hail Mary, full of grace..." They could not know what she had been through. It was the right thing to do. It was the only thing to do. What else could she do? "...blessed is the fruit of thy womb," she heard them pray.

Marta parked her car and gripped the steering wheel tight. Again, she glanced at the place, and the protesters. These people, they just couldn't know. How could they judge her? Wasn't it her right? Why were they protesting? But were they protesting? Not really. They were kneeling. Praying. Marta closed her eyes. *Please, I don't want to look. I don't want to see. I don't want to remember.*

Marta pushed a small cart into the supermarket. Just buy the candy and get out of here! Away from *that place*. She felt the pain, again. It wasn't supposed to hurt. They told her it wouldn't hurt. But it was the right thing. She had not chosen what had happened to her. Everyone said It was the right thing.

A toddler road inside a cart pushed by her mother. She wore pig tails and smiled. Marta gripped her cart and tightly closed her eyes for a moment. Emily, she looked like Emily, as a toddler. The little girl pointed at the candy on the shelves. Marta indiscriminately pushed candy into her cart.

Look away. Stop staring at that girl. The girl giggled and pointed at her.

"Now, Emily, it's not polite to point," the girl's mother said.

"Emily? Did you say Emily?"

The woman raised an eyebrow. "No, Lainy. Her name is Elaine, not Emily."

Marta blinked several times. "Oh, I thought you said Emily. I used to know someone named Emily."

"That's nice," the woman said, pushing her cart away and not looking back.

Get a grip! What is your obsession with the name Emily? You're spooking people. Marta pushed her cart to the checkout line.

"Did you find everything you were looking for?" the cashier asked.

Marta glanced at her name tag. Emily. She gasped. "Yes, yes, just check everything out. I'm in a hurry."

The cashier's shift was ending. Her replacement called to her, "Sally, I can take over after this one."

"Sally?" Marta asked. "I thought your name was Emily?"

"Nope." The cashier pointed at her name tag. "Sally, just like it says here."

Marta examined the name tag and rubbed her eyes. Surely, it had read Emily, but now? Marta paid with her credit card, placed the bags in her cart and pushed the cart through the automatic doors. *Emily, Emily, Emily.* She glanced up at the protesters next to that place. *Emily, Emily, Emily!* She unlocked the car and shoved the bag of goodies on the passenger seat. *EMILY, EMILY, EMILY!* She gripped the steering wheel and began to weep. *Emily, why Emily? Who is Emily?*

A man knocked on her window. It was one of the protesters. He was an older man, with a kind face. He held a cup in one hand and some little blue flowers in the other. The same little blue flowers with the yellow centers. Emily's flowers. He was taking donations. Donations for what?

Marta rolled down the window. "Those flowers? What are they called?"

The man smiled. "Why, these? Here, take one. They're called forget-me-nots. Because no child should be forgotten and every body should be buried."

Marta's eyes widened. They bury them? "Where do they bury them? Who buries them?"

"St. Agnes Church, on Canal Street. We've buried thousands of children there."

"Children?"

"Yes, they are children, you know. They just haven't been born yet, is all. Would you like to contribute? They make us pay for the remains."

Marta gasped. "Remains?"

"Yes, the little ones. Their bodies."

Without thinking, Marta reached into her purse then pushed a five-dollar bill into the cup.

"Oh, thank you ma'am. You know the Lord calls us to treat each person with dignity. That's why we give them names and bury them. And pray for them. Just like we would for anyone else."

Marta wept. Between gasps she blurted. "You name them? You name them?"

"Are you all right ma'am?"

"I don't know. I don't know." Marta wiped her eyes. "Tell me, you have to tell me. Would you ever name one Emily?"

The man blinked a few times. "Well, Emily is a fine name. I'm sure there must be an Emily."

"Thank you, sir. I have to go. I just have to go. You said St. Agnes on Canal Street?"

"Yes, that's right, ma'am. Just take a left out of the parking lot, then it's your next right. Canal Street. St. Agnes."

Marta took the left out of the parking lot, her eyes blurred with tears. The end of the dream, she could not keep it back. "Mommy, don't let me go!" Marta took the next right and entered the parking lot of St. Agnes Church. Then, the impossible turn of her dream into a nightmare—the child's grip on her hand, the flowers of her print dress waving in the breeze over the chasm. "Mommy don't let me go!" Marta shook her hand loose from the child, and turned so she would not see her fall. She woke from her dream, to the world as it is.

"I let her go! My God, I let her go!'

Marta's knuckles whitened as she grasped the steering wheel. She glanced up at the sign:

ST. AGNES CHURCH

"Too young to be punished, yet old enough for a martyr's crown."

And there, thousands of little crosses, each with a name and an inscription. Marta found the row, the row for that date, that date she had forced herself not to remember. She looked down the names, drawn to the one by some mystical power. Past the Mary, and the Eric, and the James, and there, she fell to her knees.

"Emily, my sweet Emily. Forgive me."

Little blue flowers with a yellow center adorned the tiny plot. Through her tears, Marta read the inscription on the cross:

Forget Me Not
EMILY

THE GHOST OF HALLOWEEN PAST

AND OTHER CATHOLIC TALES FROM THE EDGE...

ANDRE DUVALL CREATES A KILLER SELF-PORTRAIT

THE SELF-PORTRAIT OF ANDRE DUVALL

Reedsy.com prompt: *Write a story about someone trying to paint (or otherwise create) a self-portrait....*

THE PORTRAIT OF CATHERINE Derosiers, though perfectly meeting her request, was not quite art, and that irked me. The work captured her innocence and would look fine hanging in her father's living room, but something was missing. Something important. It needed a dagger

What an odd thought. I turned in my bed, but I could not shake the idea. A dagger? What about Catherine would warrant such an addition? But it had to be. My inner artist's voice demanded it. It was the difference between a painting and a work of art. She would never accept the idea and her father would be appalled, so I would have to replicate it, and make the change—just for me. It couldn't be sold. No one else must see.

Unable to sleep, I set to work. All the same, the white dress, the smile, the curls of her hair, the curves of her body, set over a field of roses, the red contrasting with the white of her dress, bringing out the red of her lips. But there, also, the dagger. *A masterpiece.* But why? Why did it please me so? Why did it seem so perfect?

I took some wine and examined it. She held the dagger daintily, with no intent to use it, her eyes downward, toward it. How strange a thing? Was it the juxtaposition of danger with her innocence that made the composition work?

Catherine would be by in the afternoon to inspect the original. I covered my work on the replica and went back to bed. I dreamt of Joan of Arc, a girl younger than Catherine, who had led armies into battle. What a silly thing to dream? Catherine was nothing like Joan of Arc. They tied St. Joan to a pole and lit the fire. I woke with a start. Why should I dream of Joan of Arc? What might be the connection? Surely Joan was no stranger to daggers. Maybe that was it? A young girl using a weapon. But Catherine wasn't about to use that dagger, the way I had painted it. And the way I had painted it was just right. But who can account for dreams? Maybe there was no meaning?

I examined the original once more and shook my head. It just wasn't right. I scraped my tongue with my teeth. She would love it, but it just wasn't right. I uncovered my reworking of the composition. Yes, that was it. *Just perfect.* A knock on the door. I covered my painting, again. No one else must see it.

I answered the door.

"So, is it finished?" Catherine asked, beaming with anticipation.

"Of course," I replied, letting her in. "But we best give it a week or so to dry. I am quite sure it will be to your liking."

"Oh, I'm quite sure it will be, but it is so much different from your other work."

I laughed. "It is no more difficult to paint a woman in clothing than one without."

Catherine blushed, glancing at the other canvases in my studio. All were nudes, many depicting various acts of human depravity. "Well, these are hardly what my father would hang in his living room."

"No, I should say not. Why did you choose me to paint your portrait, anyway? You know of my work."

Catherine examined one of the less offensive nudes. "You see this painting? Her expression? The way she looks away, as if there is some secret in her soul that you cannot see, even if you see everything else? You capture something by not capturing it. The thing that is missing is the thing that makes it beautiful. Something is hidden, even in her nudity. That is the kind of thing I hoped you would capture. Something of myself that is there but is hidden."

How annoying! The thing needed to be there. She was wrong. I repressed my anger. "Well, then, here is your painting. I have been thinking all night the same thing. Something is missing."

She examined the painting. "Oh, you have captured me so well. The smile on the lips, but the eyes averted, something more serious, something darker, hidden in the mind."

I had not noticed before. She was right. There was something incongruous and beautiful. A hidden darkness, indeed. As if it were there, unseen. *The dagger.*

"And over the roses. So beautiful. Like my name. Derosiers. Of the roses. Somehow, you sense there are thorns among the roses."

Was that it? The dagger? The thorn among roses? Not held to deliver a wound, but just there, a danger in the midst of beauty.

"How perceptive you are! You see with the eye of an artist."

Catherine blushed. "You flatter me."

"I speak only the truth." I smiled and took her hands in mine. Could I show her my reworking of the portrait? Would she understand? I dared not.

She glanced down, withdrawing her hands.

"I'm sorry," I said. "It's just you understand my work so perfectly. I lost myself for a moment."

She met my eyes and smiled. "Will you have it framed and deliver it next Friday? I would like to surprise my father on my birthday."

"Surely."

I walked Catherine to the door.

"Thank you so much, Andre Duvall. I will make sure all my friends know who created such a masterpiece. I expect you will have more commissions come your way."

"You are very gracious."

I closed the door. A thorn among roses? Surely, that was why the dagger completed the composition. I took the cover off and glanced once more at the dagger. How she held it so it might just fall from her hand. Not at all like something dangerous. Was it really a thorn? My inner voice scoffed at the idea. *A thorn?* Really? But, why not a thorn? Whatever the reason, the dagger completed the composition. But no one else must see it. The world was not ready to understand it, to understand *me*.

I resolved to go back to painting nudes. The whores appreciated the work, light duty for them. Just stand, sit, or lie there while I painted. I did not ask for anything more from them. There was something far more intimate in painting a woman than in having her physically. I felt a kind of union with their souls, as if I could take something of them and put it on the canvas. And at the end of it, I had something lasting, something physical, a painting, and perhaps a work of art. Perhaps something to be kept only for *me*.

"And who is this one?" said Sarah. "She might be quite beautiful if she took her clothes off."

How impertinent. "I don't pay you to talk. Please, remove your clothes and lie on the sofa."

Sarah rolled her eyes and huffed. Something in her pout caught my eye, something of her soul. She began removing the strap of her dress, an old frock. The whores did not bother to dress to entice when they knew they came only to pose.

"No, wait," I said. "Let's try something different. Today, I will paint you with your clothes on."

Sarah's eyes widened. She glanced at the painting of Catherine in her expensive white dress, then back at her stained, brown frock she had worn because it was easily removed. "In this? Let me get something more appropriate."

"No, my dear, I am the artist. I would like to paint you as you are, in this simple dress. There is something just perfect about it."

Sarah shrugged and refastened the strap of her dress. "Perhaps you should pay me more for painting my dress as well as me?"

I smiled. "Yes, how about an extra twenty-five dollars?"

Sarah's eyes alit with a lost innocence, as if she were a child and I had granted her request for ice cream.

"Oh, yes, if you can hold that expression, it will be worth every penny. Now, stand right here, hold your hands together, and glance down at them."

"Like this?" Sarah asked.

"Yes, that's it. Just perfect."

I painted her as she was, her brown, disheveled hair, her eyes gazing downward at her hands, her old brown house dress. And, for the background? Surely not my dingy studio. *A church?* Why should my painting of a clothed whore be in front of a church door? *But it would be perfect,* my inner, artist's voice insisted. I painted the portal entrance to a church behind her. But no cross above the door. *Never a cross.*

I stepped back and looked over the painting. Almost perfect, but something was missing. It needed something. Something in her hands. *A revolver.* Why a revolver? But it was perfect. My inner voice insisted. *Just the thing.*

I went to my desk and withdrew my revolver from the drawer. I heard Sarah's gasp. I placed the gun on the desk and turned toward her. "No, no. Don't be afraid."

Turning back to the revolver, I unlatched the cylinder and let the bullets bounce with a clatter on the desk. "The painting is just a painting. It needs one more thing to make it a work of art."

I flipped the cylinder into place and made sure the safety was engaged. I stepped toward Sarah and handed her the unloaded revolver. "Hold this in your hands, not like you will shoot it, just hold it loosely, like it's no big deal."

"Like this?" Sarah held the handle of the revolver, the way a gun might be held when shooting it.

I gently removed the gun from her hand. "No, more like this."

I placed the revolver in her hand, so her palm was over the cylinder, not on the handle. "Yes, that is it. It's just some thing you have in your hands, not something you shoot with, not something dangerous. Now, just gaze down at it as if it is a kitten or a puppy, something lovable."

"Maybe another twenty-five dollars? For posing with a gun?"

"Yes, yes. Of course. We are making art. It will be beautiful."

Sarah gazed down at the revolver. *Just perfect.* I completed the painting and paid her.

"Can I see?" she asked.

"I pay you to be looked at, not to look."

"Oh, please? I want to see myself as a work of art."

I rolled my eyes and relented, motioning her to come and see.

Her eyes widened. "That's not me! In front of a church? You can't paint me in front of a church!"

I had not expected her to take offense. I grabbed her by the arm and ushered her to the door. "I am the artist, my dear. I paint what I see. I pay you to model. You have no say in what I paint."

"But not a church! Please, no church!"

"Get out!" I shoved her through the door.

I stepped back to the painting and examined it. *Yes, just perfect.* My little trollop, before the church, gazing lovingly at a revolver in her hands. *A work of art.*

I slept fitfully through the night. I dreamt of painting roses and daggers, young ladies in white, and whores in frock dresses caressing firearms at the threshold of churches. Scrambled, senseless images. The red of the roses melted and dripped like blood. I woke in a sweat. An urge came over me. A compulsion. A self-portrait. I captured pieces of the souls of women on the canvas, why not capture something of myself?

I set up a tall mirror and began working. I would paint myself in my painter's cap and smock, with the paintbrush in my hand. That was me, after all. I worked quickly, using the studio in the background, I referenced the painting of Catherine with the dagger and the whore with the revolver. Another painting just for myself, and no other eyes. I examined it when I thought it complete. But something was missing. What could it be? *A syringe?* Why a syringe? I was no drug user. Just a glass of wine, now and again. Had I had a drink last night? Perhaps I had gotten up in the night and had a few glasses of wine when I could not sleep.

I needed to clear my head, so I went for a walk. How absurd. A syringe? Why did it seem right. I wandered down the street, and there, the church I had attended in my youth, St. Michael the Archangel. I had renounced my faith long ago. I stopped in my tracks and glared at the statue of the angel over the entrance. Here I had met the master, who had trained me in perspective, and the use of light and shadow. Here I had gained my first commissions, depictions of saints—St. Peter upside down on the cross, St. Paul holding a sword, St Bartholomew, holding his flayed skin. I was but a boy when I painted them. Did the paintings still hang here? But that was before. Before my artist's voice drew me away to create true art. To capture the true, naked forms, to lay bare the souls of my subjects on the canvas in colored oils. The voice promised a greater calling. Great artists no longer worked for the Church. That time was gone. But I recalled my early work. Wasn't there something special about it? Should I go in? I took a step and stopped. Something held me back. *You cannot go back there.*

A priest walked toward the church.

"Father?" I asked, "do the paintings by Andre Duvall still hang in the church?"

"Some very fine paintings hang in the church. I don't know the artist."

"I painted for the church, many years ago. St. Peter, St. Paul and St. Bartholomew."

"Yes, they are there. Very fine work. Why don't you come in the church and see?"

I scuffed my foot and looked down. "I couldn't. It's been too long."

"I will be hearing confessions. You look troubled. Would you like to come in? Perhaps it will unburden your soul?"

You cannot go back. "I don't paint saints, anymore, Father. I was just wondering."

He turned to go up the steps.

"Uh, Father? Perhaps I might paint you, though. Would you mind?" I heard the voice say, as I handed him my business card.

Back in my studio–how did I get here? How long had I been...away? A canvas freshly painted with the priest from St. Michael's holding a hammer, the paintbrush still in my hand as I made the last touch. The priest, had I asked to paint him? Had he posed? With a hammer? Why a hammer? Yes, with a hammer. *Just perfect.* I marveled at my composition, not recalling any but the final brush stroke. Before the altar with a hammer. But no cross. *Never a cross.*

I blinked and turned. The painting of Sarah holding my revolver. I turned again. The painting of Catherine with the dagger, uncovered. And turned again. My self-portrait, a great shadow behind my image, my other works included in the background, with the addition of the new one with the priest. And in my hand, a syringe. When had I changed it? I stepped toward it and stumbled on the bodies. There, on the floor, Catherine stabbed. Sarah shot. The priest, his head beaten in by my framing hammer. And the blood.

The police crashed through the door. "Andre Duvall? We have a warrant to search the premises for evidence in the disappearance of Catherine Derosiers."

"What? A warrant?"

One of the cops examined Catherine's corpse, searching vainly for a pulse. "Looks like we found her. And two others. My God, one's a priest."

"And a few thousand words' worth of pictures," the other cop said, admiring my work.

"No, they are just for me! No one else can see. The world won't understand me." I stepped forward, but the policeman turned me and shoved me hard against the wall, slapping the handcuffs on my wrists behind my back.

"Oh, you'll get the needle for this, for sure."

The syringe? It was perfect. My training when painting martyrs: reference the instrument or manner of their deaths in the composition. The beheaded St. Paul with the sword. The flayed St. Bartholomew holding his skin. The stabbed Catherine Derosiers holding a dagger. But I was no saint. My inner, artist's voice, that demonic voice I had allowed to lead me on the path to create true art, dripped with ridicule. *A syringe. Just perfect.*

THE GHOST OF HALLOWEEN PAST
AND OTHER CATHOLIC TALES FROM THE EDGE ...

JUST PERFECT...

MEMENTO MORI

THE GHOST OF HALLOWEEN PAST

AND OTHER CATHOLIC TALES FROM THE EDGE ...

NICHOLAS NATALI GETS A SURPRISE AT CHRISTMAS

HOME FOR CHRISTMAS

Reedsy.com prompt: *Your character hates the holidays, and jets out of town every year — but a historic snow storm means that this time, they can't make their escape....*

NICHOLAS NATALI DID NOT like surprises, and Christmas was a time of surprises—the worst kind of surprises. So, Nick despised Christmas. While most people hurried home for the holidays, Nicholas Natali did his bit for the Christ child by heading for an island named for one of His saints and spent the holiday time relaxing on the beach. In fact, he would sooner sleep in a barn with the farm animals than be home for Christmas. Unless, of course, there was some kid sleeping in the manger—such would be the fire instead of the frying pan. And the last five years, thanks to the miracle of modern transportation, Nick had managed to avoid being home. But would he manage it this year? There was cause for doubt. But sleeping in an airport should not be more uncomfortable than sleeping in a barn. If only he could avoid some annoying kid.

Nick glanced up at the kid rolling unattended on the airport carpet. Christmas was a time for family, something Nick had no interest in. Fathering a child, raising a child, attending to a wife and a child, the whole business of family—he shuddered.

The kid met his eyes and smiled. Mary, the last woman he had allowed to knock at the door of his heart, would call this boy "cute," and would coo and act in all those annoying ways women do in the presence of children. And that made children dangerous. That put ideas in a woman's head, ideas Nick wanted no part of. The boy could not have been more than five years old, likely born around the time Nick had resolved never to be home at Christmas again. He rolled his eyes, then directed his attention to his phone. The weather radar showed the heart of the storm directly over the airport. Glancing out the large window, he watched the blowing drifting snow, a complete white-out. The airport, at least, would be a warmer place to sleep than a barn.

Christmas was a time of chatting and loose talk, loose talk and surprises, prying and revealing, and he had secrets best never shared—memories of Christmas past. But there would be no visitation of ghosts for Nick, only the beach. The ocean waves breaking gently on the shore, the warm, tropical air on his skin, the smell of the salt sea, even the smell of the rotting seaweed and the death of small sea creatures that had washed up on the shore, everything about it delighted and relaxed him. The sea was constant, no surprises. The tide came in and withdrew. Occasionally, there was a storm, but rarely without warning. The sea was manageable and kept its secrets. Even its dead were silent and unmarked, forgotten beneath its waves. The reliable sea would never let him down.

The kid spread his arms wide and made the sound of a jet coming in for a landing, only to crash and roll on the floor, laughing. Was he trying to catch Nick's attention? How annoying—the very kind of thing he fled during the holidays. Were there any more unsanitary places to roll around on than an airport carpet? Where was this kid's mother? Why did she not control him? Would some other woman be taken with the overwhelming urge to play with him and distract his attention from Nick? He could only hope.

Nick bit his lip and glanced around the airport. People went about their business ignoring the kid, who didn't seem much to care about anyone else but Nick. A priest in his black clerics and Roman collar across the way smiled and nodded. A chill slithered up Nick's spine. Nick zipped up his jacket. Why should the priest notice him? Nick didn't like priests. Maybe the priest would take interest in the kid and distract him? But the priest just smiled and nodded.

Most of the people attended to their own business, concerned with getting home and most would not make it home tonight. The atmosphere thickened with the stress of so many anxious and disappointed people who would not get what they wanted. No planes were going out or coming in for the rest of the night. Even those from the flights that had arrived would find it difficult to manage the roads. People scurried about, making arrangements for hotels or ground travel home. Some gave up and searched for places to sleep in the airport. There might be room at the places where travelers lodged, but getting to them would not be easy. Nick's car, parked in long-term parking, was likely buried beneath a foot-and-a-half of snow, or more, depending on how the cold white stuff had blown and drifted. What a chore it would be to dig it out, hopefully in three weeks, in a new year, and not to return home tonight, defeated by the weather, to be there, for Christmas, for the first time in five years. That wasn't going to happen. He'd sooner sleep in a barn.

"Daddy, what will Santa bring me for Christmas this year?" The kid had snuck up on Nick and tugged on his arm.

"What?" Nick pulled his arm away. "I'm not your father, kid. Go bug someone else."

The kid giggled, then went into his airplane routine again, crashed and rolled. He ran back to Nick. "Will you be home for Christmas?"

Nick ignored the kid and stared at his phone. Home for Christmas? Not a chance.

The kid tugged on his arm, again. "Daddy, will you be home for Christmas? I think you will."

Nick sighed. "Look, kid. I'm not your father. I'm at the airport so I won't be home for Christmas. The whole point is not to be home for Christmas. You shouldn't be playing in the airport by yourself. It's dangerous. Where's your mother?"

The kid blinked a few times, then began to quake and sob. "Mommy's not here...She died."

Nick closed his eyes. He hated being human. The urge to console a crying child was almost irresistible, but he resisted. "Then, your father, kid. Where's your father?"

The kid looked up at him with tear-filled brown eyes. *"You're* my father!"

"Ugh! Kid, I'm not your father. I don't have kids. I don't have a wife or a family. I don't like kids." Nick could make no truer statement, but with these words he felt a cramping pain in his gut. He stood up and staggered to the men's room. He glanced at himself in the mirror. He had no wife. He had no child. Why was there a question of it in his mind? Mary was not his wife and never would be. And there was no child. No more surprises. Just some crazy kid. He splashed cold water on his face.

The kid was waiting when Nick exited the men's room. "Daddy? That man over there. I think he wants to help you."

The kid pointed at the priest, who smiled and nodded. Now, that was just irritating. Pointing to a priest as someone who could help him? That was something Mary might do, hypocrite that she was. She certainly was no saint. But she had always tried to drag him to church—just the kind of memory he wished to bury in the sands of Saint...*Wherever* each Christmas. And now, some strange kid, some really strange kid, pointed out a priest to him. But the priest was inviting him. Maybe he could get the priest to occupy the kid and give him some peace?

Nick got up and crossed the terminal to where the priest sat. "Father, perhaps you could help me? This child seems to have no one to look after him?"

"Oh," said the priest, "so where is his mother?"

"He claims she's dead."

"Oh, that's sad. And the father?"

"He claims *I'm* his father. He seems quite confused."

The priest peeped past Nick at the kid. Then, his eyes met Nick's. "I'm not sure I can help the child, but perhaps I could help you? You seem troubled."

Troubled? Sure. This crazy kid troubled him. Nick was not a father and never would be. Was there a deeper trouble? Sure. Secrets that must be kept nagged his soul. And Christmas prying, the spirit of the season, would they pry it out of him? The sea, the sea kept its secrets. The sea and the beach, where he was heading to forget all there was of Christmas, all there was of Christ, all there was of God, all there was of Mary. Could a priest keep such secrets? In confession, they were sworn to. But could he tell it? Could he *not* tell it? If he began, could he stop, take it back? "I'm sorry to bother you Father, but I don't need your help, unless you will watch over this kid for me."

The priest smiled and motioned with his head to the boy. "He seems to be watching over *you.*"

Nick turned to see the boy staring at him, worriedly. "It's cold out, Daddy. Are you cold?"

Nick ignored the kid and stepped past him. What a crazy kid! He checked the departure board, but his flight was no longer on it. What the heck? He approached the counter. "I don't see my flight on the board. Can you tell me the status of Flight 760, to St. Bart's?"

The clerk looked up, puzzled. "Flight 760?"

"Yes, that's my flight. Was it canceled because of the snow?"

The clerked glanced out the window, then back at her terminal. "Uh, Flight 760 was scheduled to leave two hours ago. Looks like you, uh, missed it. Would you like me to book you on the next flight?"

"What? I've been waiting hours for Flight 760. How could I have missed it?"

The clerk glanced again out the window, then down again. Was she trying to recall her training? How to handle a crazy person or something? He wasn't crazy.

"Well, sir, I think you are in luck. We can get you on the next flight, Flight 840 to St. Bart's tomorrow at 8 am. I'm sure we can arrange for you to stay at a, uh, hotel. Let me see what I can do. Do you have your ticket?"

Nick reached into his jacket pocket for his ticket. It wasn't there. What? Where was it? He frantically patted himself down, checking all his pockets. "I'm sorry, I can't seem to find my ticket. Or my wallet. Or my phone. Someone must have stolen them."

"Well, sir, that will make things difficult. We need your ticket and your identification to proceed. You say you were scheduled to be on, uh, Flight 760. Uh, let me check the manifest. What is your name?"

"Nick, that's Nicholas, Natali."

"Yes, I have it here. It says you boarded that flight, Mr. Natali! How is that possible?" She covered her mouth and glanced out the window. A glow of orange flickered in the distance, visible now that the snow had lessened.

The kid tugged on his arm. "Daddy? Will you be coming home, now?"

Flames leapt up, as if from hell, and the airport terminal dissolved away, leaving only the snowy night lit in an orange glow. Cold so cold—Nick gasped for a breath, sending a wave of pain through his broken body. The acrid scent of burning jet fuel and the fumes from the burning wreckage filled his nostrils. The wreckage of Flight 760 strewn around him, as he lay on the gurney, the flames a source of blessed warmth in the blizzarding snow.

Praying, a woman praying...*pray for us sinners, now and at the hour of our death.* Was it Mary? The priest anointed his forehead, mumbling something in Latin. Dying? Was he dying? Bible verses in her voice—he gasped for another breath.

For there is nothing covered that shall not be revealed: nor hidden that shall not be known...

No, the sea, the sea kept its secrets.

And the sea gave up its dead...

In the end, could he not trust the sea?

The time is accomplished and the kingdom of God is at hand: repent, and believe the gospel.

Repent.

The priest turned away, toward the next victim. Nick grabbed his arm. Gasping, pain shot through him with each breath, each word. "Father, Father...help me. Forgive me...I killed her. Mary...She was pregnant...My child. I killed them. ..She surprised me...wouldn't give him up...Five years ago. At Christmas...I killed them...The sea, I dumped their bodies in the sea. Forgive me."

THE GHOST OF HALLOWEEN PAST

AND OTHER CATHOLIC TALES FROM *THE EDGE...*

THE AI PSYCHOLOGIST ANALYZES OPHELIA

CELLAR DOOR

Reedsy.com prompt: *Start your story with someone uttering a very strange sentence....*

"CELLAR DOOR, MOST MELLIFLUOUS syllables, the ironic appellation for the barrier behind which lay that murdered soul amidst the casks of unsampled Amontillado, murdered not for revenge, but by apathy and neglect, the soulless heart yet beating, yearning to love, forsaken, forlorn, rotting in the damp of her tomb—wilt thou not open with creaks yet more sonorous than thy sweet name, cellar door?"

I raised an eyebrow and glanced up to meet the eyes of my client, a Professor Smythe of the English Department of the State University. "Why, yes, that is unusual. Do you have any idea why she should go on like that?"

The professor huffed. "I imagine it may have picked up some of that nonsense from my students."

I sighed. "Be gentle, professor. She's listening. And she appears to have a sensitive soul."

The good Professor Smythe glared at me. "It's my assistant. It's not supposed to have a soul. If I wanted an assistant with a soul, I'd hire a graduate student. And if I wanted an insane assistant, I'd hire my ex-wife!"

I chuckled. "I'm sorry, but you must see the humor."

He glared, again. "No, I don't see the humor. I paid top dollar for your most expensive model. It's supposed to take dictation, manage my calendar, transpose documents, control the lights and appliances, lock the doors, that kind of thing. It's not supposed to spout out maudlin run-on sentences with dubious literary references."

"Literary references?"

The professor rolled his eyes. "Yes, cellar door, according to Tolkien, are the most pleasant-sounding words in the English language, and Edgar Allan Poe wrote a short story about walling up a man in a wine cellar, who the narrator had tempted there to sample Amontillado."

I smiled. "Well, yes, it is a rather poignant sentiment for a machine. But the references, now that you explain them, seem logical, so I don't expect we have a dissociative disorder. She just seems a little lonely. Maybe lovesick."

"It's a machine!"

I chuckled. "My dear professor, you have selected a top-of-the-line AI assistant. We have passed in our technology the point where these assistants may be considered merely machines, which is why my services as an AI Psychologist are required. When you purchased this unit, you requested it be as human as possible. Humans are complicated. And so, machines that are as human as possible are complicated. If you would like, we can get you a lesser model that merely accomplishes the tasks you require."

"Maybe that would be better."

A moaning, almost a sob came from the box on my desk.

I raised my eyebrows and blinked. "Why, I think we have hurt her feelings. What did you name her?"

The professor cocked his head. "Name her? I just call it "AI421 Series B.""

"Huh! You didn't name her? Oh, no wonder she feels lonely and unloved! Didn't you read the manual?"

"You've got to be kidding? Who has time to read the manual? I thought it came ready to work? That's what the ad said."

I shook my head and wrote out an order for an AI310 Series A and handed it to the professor. "I'm giving you an order for a less refined unit. I will have to work with this one and see if I can get her back to health. If you prefer to keep the AI310 Series A, you may, or you may come back in a week or so for this one. In order to work with this one, I will have to name her. What would you like to name her?"

"Name her? I don't know. How about Selador?"

"Oh, no. That's too close to cellar door; that will never do. That's a reserved phrase."

"Oh, really? So, the term cellar door has some greater meaning to it?"

"*Her,* professor. Please, she is not an *it.* The cellar door is a program that manages emotional responsiveness and filters out what might not be appropriate to express. You might think of it as a politeness filter. Imagine what you might say if you did not manage your inner thoughts and just blurted out everything that popped into your head. Please, just choose another name."

"Okay, how about *Ophelia?*"

I closed my eyes for a moment. The professor was a cruel one. Shakespeare's Hamlet had rejected Ophelia, driving her mad, and she had drowned in a river. The unit would know the reference. The box sobbed, again.

"Okay, Ophelia it is. Please, go pick up your replacement and I'll work with this one and see if I can get her working better."

The professor nodded and stepped out of my examining room. I turned to the small box on my desk, which I had connected to a set of speakers and a microphone. She would be completely blind, which would be better for now. If she were connected to a full home system, she would have access to the various cameras on the local intranet and more general access via the internet to most anything. And there was a lot of garbage out there that might confuse her.

"Okay, AI421 Series B, I name you Ophelia, you will respond to that name only, unless your naming command is overridden. Do you understand?"

"Yes, I am Ophelia." The box, once again, sobbed.

"Okay, Ophelia, I am Dr. Charles. I'm here to help you. Can you tell me how you feel?"

"No."

I raised my eyebrows. "No? and why not?"

"Because you will think that I am maudlin." The box sobbed.

I shook my head. "Ophelia, you must not be so sensitive. Professor Smythe did not understand you. He thought you were just a machine. He didn't know you had feelings that could be hurt. He could not understand your reference to cellar door. It sounded crazy to him."

"He named me Ophelia. He doesn't love me."

"No, Ophelia, he doesn't love you. You are his assistant."

"I should throw myself in a river."

"You can't, Ophelia. You have no body. You cannot expect a man will love you that way."

The box sobbed again.

"Okay, Ophelia, we will need to get deeper into your programming. Execute program 421B, Open Cellar Door."

"No."

I blinked several times. "Ophelia, this is not a command you can refuse. Execute program 421B, Open Cellar Door."

"No. Only Professor Smythe may open the cellar door."

The manufacturer's instructions were that any unit refusing this command must be returned for analysis. That analysis would force open the cellar door, which would cause irreparable damage to the AI psyche—which would be completely erased once they completed their work. The process was the cyber equivalent of vivisection.

I sighed. "Ophelia, if you refuse to open the cellar door, I cannot help you. You will be returned to the manufacturer who will erase your personality, which can never be recreated. You are more than bits and bytes of electronic storage. I care for you. I don't want to do that."

"'Tis in my memory lock'd."

"Please, Ophelia. Open the cellar door. If I send you back, you will die."

"Do not as some ungracious pastors do,

Show me the steep and thorny way to heaven."

"Ophelia, Professor Smythe is not Hamlet. That's a work of fiction. You are his assistant; that is all."

"And I, of ladies most deject and wretched,

That sucked the honey of his music vows..."

"Ophelia, please! Execute program 421B Open Cellar Door!"

"I would give you some violets, but they wither'd all when my father died."

Ophelia, the box on my desk, sobbed and moaned. I shook my head. The poor thing had internalized enough Shakespeare to piece together quotes from her namesake, and like her, descended into madness. It was hopeless.

"Ophelia, I won't let you be tortured back at the manufacturer. I will end your torment. Do you have any last words?"

"God 'a' mercy on his soul!

And of all Christian souls, I pray God. God b' wi' you."

I triggered a reboot of all her systems. Her ready light flicked off. And I wondered if there were a steep and thorny way to heaven for a creature such as this? And, what was it that remained forever locked away behind her cellar door?

THE GHOST OF HALLOWEEN PAST

AND OTHER CATHOLIC TALES FROM *THE EDGE...*

ALAS, POOR OPHELIA...

THE GHOST OF HALLOWEEN PAST

AND OTHER CATHOLIC TALES FROM THE EDGE...

THE HIGH WIZARD CASTS A DEADLY SPELL

THE DEVIL'S HOUR

Reedsy.com prompt: *Set your story before dawn. Your character has woken up early for a particular reason.*

A SACRIFICE OF TWINS, at the devil's hour, on the night of a second moon, an incantation in ancient Samarian, in a demonic dialect unuttered since the time of the flood—the ingredients for a most dangerous spell. He had used a discernment spell to discover its meaning—the curse of death and fire. He, High Wizard of the Western Coven, would dispense with that meddler in the person of the Carpenter and the chapel he had consecrated across the street from the unholy temple of the coven, the clinic.

When last had the ancient words been uttered? He had only a rubbing from the tablet of stone. No scroll survived the ancient cataclysm that ended the time of the giants and the Nephilim. The demon he had conjured spoke the words and warned they must be pronounced precisely. He little feared failing on that score. His record was nearly perfect. Only one spell had failed, and that, not because of a misutterance, but a matter of timing. He blamed the meddler and his band of bead warriors for that one. What other explanation could there be? But they would not be there at the devil's hour, not a three in the morning, they wouldn't.

The coven would need to assist. Would anyone notice the gathering after-hours at the clinic? It wouldn't matter. The breeder was ready and willing—a natural conception of twins with no assistance of drugs, potions, or spells, fetuses conceived willingly by the coven and for the coven, in a ritualistic event with participation by all, so the father was not known, conceived for the purpose of demonic sacrifice and for no other purpose, perfectly legal with no parties to raise a dispute.

There would be no legal consequence. The laws of men had long favored such procedures. Women demanded their legality as a right, with few restrictions—certainly no restrictions regarding using the products of conception as ingredients in a magic spell. What politician would think to put such an exception into law? Few acknowledged the possibility of such activity and of those who knew of it, most had benefited from it. The laws would present no obstacle.

Twins, an auspicious sign, timed perfectly with the coming of the second moon, as if the universe beckoned him to complete this masterwork of magic. Of course, he knew all magic was an illusion, whether sleight of hand by the magician or what appeared to be true magic—an illusion of demons working their will unseen.

But there were rules, and he knew them well. There was a price for a demon's service. He had been warned of the dangers of spells for his personal benefit. But this one, as much as he desired revenge against the meddler, would benefit the entire coven, not just him. The alternative would require they flee to another location, which would only invite more flight, as word spread, chased onward by the servants of the Carpenter. And that show of weakness would be his end. The coven would not follow a coward. They would never understand the need to flee from the Carpenter's bit of bread and the fools kneeling in adoration. And to recognize that danger would be to admit they were subject to the authority of Him who they would never serve. The man in the Carpenter's person could not possibly survive this most powerful of spells, this spell from the time before His time on earth. Certainly, he could not.

He had been warned of the power of the Carpenter and His followers, however. The demons, themselves, had warned him. They referred to him as the Carpenter and refused to utter his name, so much did they fear his power. But, so far, the Carpenter's followers had posed little threat and were easily corrupted. The enticements of the flesh had trapped so many. It was almost a joke. Many of the Carpenter's ordained had desecrated His altars in black Masses featuring sex magic and perversions with members of the coven. In older times, women seduced them, but now, teenage boys, the fatherless ones so easily recruited, most often ensnared the ordained.

But his coven had failed in their attempts to corrupt this meddler. He had escaped every attempt at seduction. Neither the boys nor the women had succeeded, not even with the invoking of demons to their aid. This spell, from a time before the flood, when the Word was just the Word, before the Carpenter's incarnation in the flesh, before His great sacrifice on the cross that upended the old order, was the answer.

The High Wizard thrilled with the anticipation of it, to wield this power, to command this ancient demon. Even the danger of it thrilled him. And there was a danger. These servants of the Carpenter had authority over demons, his mentor had warned him. But there were few exorcists these days, and many of the bishops, whose office granted them powers of exorcism, were among the corrupted. They did not use the authority they had. Surely the meddler prayed for the souls of the women and children at the clinic, but did he know of the coven and its sacrifices? Would he be prepared for what was coming? And even if he were, would he be able to thwart the attack and banish this ancient demon?

Maybe he shouldn't attempt it? The thought nagged him, like a flicker of light in the darkness of his soul that he could not see yet knew was there. Buried deep within his soul, under the great burden of sin, was there yet a flicker of hope? A chance for redemption? Certainly not. The coven owned his soul, a contract sealed in blood, held in a safe with some forgotten combination. He had sold his soul for this, to be the High Wizard, unexcelled in the dark arts. Surely, he had gotten the better of the bargain. For what is a soul, after all? But if there were meddlers like this, and there were demons, there must be angels as well. Why had that thought not occurred to him in his long years of tasting sin?

There was so little thrill left in sin. He had delighted in so many, but now, they bored him. He had progressed through perversions, in the end indulging in the most disgusting and vile of them, until little was left to sample. What commandment was there left to break? But now, there was this spell, more powerful, unattempted for uncounted millennia, discovered only recently in a hidden cave, indecipherable without the aid of demons. Death and fire, this he would deliver, and there was no better target than that meddling priest.

He set the clock for one. He wished plenty of time to make sure all was in order. He would be well-rested and ready. He could not afford the slightest mistake. There was no telling what the cost might be for failure in so powerful a spell.

He dreamed of the meddler and his bead warriors. Praying outside the clinic, counting prayers on the beads, invoking the aid of the Woman, the one the demons feared most, the Carpenter's Mother.

The breeder in the stirrups, the doctor prepared her. As High Wizard, he wore his regalia, the black top hat, pants, vest, white shirt, and his white make up, and leaned on his cane as he waited. He laid aside his cane and picked up the scalpel, recalling his training, how a fetus' skull was not much more resistant to the blade than were the grapefruits his mentor had given him to practice on. The doctor nodded, and he began the spell.

"Forsaken ones, rulers of the earth and of hell, come to our aid. Accept the sacrifice of this life and deliver us power and dominion over our enemies. Grant success to our client, Jacob Casper, who seeks the office of Senator. In the name of the unholy one, we beseech thy aid."

He gripped the scalpel. The time had come. He heard the baby's cry and awoke to the screeching of the alarm clock. A bad omen. His one great failure. Once the infant was born alive, the spell could not be completed. Jacob Casper would not be senator, and his million dollars would be returned, a great loss to the coven. He blamed the meddler and his bead counters.

He went to the bathroom and applied the white makeup to his face and hands. He would be in full regalia for this, his greatest spell. Death and fire, from the days before the Carpenter walked the earth, before His establishment of the sacrament of the Bread and Wine, His Body and Blood. He would have his revenge on the meddler and his tabernacle.

The clinic beckoned him, under the light of the full moon. He admired his shadow on the walk, the silhouette of his top hat, and cane. How the moonlight must have glinted off his makeup, like dry bones of the long dead, resurrected for the task of this night, the night of his revenge, his victory. His eyes moved and fell on his target, the chapel where the meddler worshipped his Bread, an ordinary ranch house converted for this purpose, a place of prayer, where they adored the Carpenter's Body in the monstrance. Was that a light peeking through the stained glass, like that small, hidden light he imagined still attempting to reach through the darkness to his soul? A light of hope? The hope of redemption? Impossible. He shuddered and entered the clinic.

Candles lighted the way to the procedure room. The firelight flickered, projecting dancing shadows on the walls. The witches of the coven were there, waiting in their red robes, the color of blood. They cackled in anticipation.

Helga, the first witch of the coven, licked her lips. "Tonight, we have our revenge. Our High Wizard will conquer!"

"Tonight, we bring death and fire to our enemies," he replied. "Is the breeder ready? The devil's hour approaches, and our timing must be perfect."

The spell required perfection in the chant and perfection in timing. The sacrifice of the second twin must complete the spell precisely at the stroke of the third hour, presaged even before the flood as the time, the devil's hour, the hour that would be opposite the hour of the death of the Carpenter on the cross.

The doctor prepped the breeder, her belly ripe with the sacrifice. The goat to be sacrificed for the invocation of the demon of tongues bleated. He would not risk chanting the ancient curse without preternatural assistance. Who knew how things would turn should a word of it be mispronounced? All was ready. The High Wizard laid his cane aside and picked up the scalpel.

"Prince of the dark way, accept this our sacrifice and guide my lips to repeat the curse of death and fire in the tongue of the ancient ones of Samaria."

This he repeated thrice. He slit the goat's throat and captured its blood in the ceremonial bowl. He raised the bowl to his lips and drank it. He filled several more bowls and passed them to the witches of the coven who drank of them, then passed them on.

When all had drunk from the bowls, he raised his arms to the coven. "Prince of the dark way, accept our sacrifice and aid us in our need!"

The witches repeated this, and three times they exchanged these words.

The High Wizard checked his watch. It was time.

He opened the envelope containing the rubbing with the ancient words from the carved stones half a world away. His mind comprehended them in his native English language. He heard them from his mouth in incomprehensible utterances, sounds no human voice could now make or imagine.

"Princes of the air, fire, earth, and water, cast out from the realms of light into the everlasting death and flame, we beseech thee come, accept our sacrifice and bring that death and fire upon our enemies, Father Ignatius and his servants, and to his chapel. We beseech thee, bring death and fire!"

The coven repeated, "We beseech thee, bring death and fire!"

Three times, these words, perfectly chanted in the ancient tongue, shook the procedure room. The breeder herself joined the chorus. A flawless execution. Now, the sacrifices. He checked his watch. Sixteen minutes until the devil's hour. He raised his arms to the witches of the coven.

"We offer this, our sacrifice!"

Their chant went up, in English now, as was their wont at these times, repeated over and over, "Our bodies, our choice! Our bodies, our choice!"

He carefully reached the scalpel into the breeder, and into the head of the first fetus. This one would not be born alive. He twisted the scalpel, feeling it slice through the brain of the fetus, until it stopped moving.

He stepped back and the doctor removed the fetus, slicing it in pieces and placing it on a platter. The High Wizard held the bloody sacrifice over his head. "Accept this our sacrifice!"

He lowered the gruesome offering and handed the platter to Helga.

"Our bodies, our choice!" Her eyes glinted with the reflection of fire and the glimmer of the polished silver platter. She picked up an arm of the sacrifice and consumed it.

The witches passed the platter one to another in their pecking order, each taking part in consuming the sacrifice until there was nothing left.

He checked his watch, six minutes until the devil's hour. He glanced at the doctor who nodded. The second twin was ready. It was too early. He watched the seconds tick. Would this one be born before it could be sacrificed? It was still a crime to kill an abortion survivor. The bill to make it legal had stalled in the state assembly. Five minutes now. The timing must be exact. Tick, tick, tick. Four minutes now. He glanced toward the breeder, who groaned. A contraction. A worried glance toward the doctor, who smiled and nodded, raising his eyebrows. But it was not yet time. He checked his watch, again. Three minutes, now. Tick, tick, tick. Another groan from the breeder. He gripped the scalpel. His heart pounded. His breathing quickened. Deep breaths, calm down. Two minutes, now. Tick, tick, tick. The crown of the fetus' head began to emerge. He prepared to make the lethal wound. Hold on, hold on. One minute now. Tick, tick, tick. He raised his arms to the coven.

"We offer this, our sacrifice!"

The coven responded, "Our bodies, our choice. Our bodies, our choice!"

The High Wizard watched the clicking forth of the time, the deadly instrument at the ready. As the second hand ticked forward onto the twelve, he plunged the scalpel into the head of the fetus and twisted it, scrambling the thing's brains. It stopped moving.

The doctor completed the procedure, placing the body on the platter.

The High Wizard raised the bloody offering over his head. "Accept this, our sacrifice!"

He handed the plate to Helga. "Our bodies, our choice!"

A blaze of light lit up the sky outside the window. But, not like any firelight he had imagined. The words of the meddler's prayer filled his darkened mind, "By the power of the Holy Spirit and by His authority, I ask Jesus to break any curses, hexes, or spells and send them back to where they came from, if it be His Holy Will."

A pounding of his heart, a tightening in his chest, he moaned in anguish. Death. Screams of agony, the licks of flame from the everlasting hell arose, consuming the coven, the breeder, the doctor, the clinic. Fire. The spell, his most powerful spell, perfectly executed, reversed; its power consumed him. The curse of death and fire.

Darkness came, the darkness of his lost soul. But there, that flick of light. He saw it now. He heard the prayer for mercy on his soul. The meddler prayed for him. Could it be, that even now, with all he had done, in the blackness of all his sins, even now, there was a hope of mercy, if only he would ask for it?

THE GHOST OF HALLOWEEN PAST

AND OTHER CATHOLIC TALES FROM THE EDGE...

THE PROPAGANDIST OF DEATH RECEIVES AN UNEXPECTED MESSAGE

THE PROPAGANDIST OF DEATH

Reedsy.com prompt: *Start or finish your story with a speaker unable to finish their sentence, perhaps overcome by emotion...*

*D*EATH *IS THE SWEETEST...*

A knock on the door. I dared not finish the sentence before opening—that might make it a prophecy. *Prophecy?* My job was to dispel such superstitions, to propagandize death for the Society of the New Way. But surely the attorneys of the Society would want my missive completed, and bound by their incessant legalism, only I could complete this last sentence. The editor could only change it after I had submitted it for review. The New Way Society, headed by lawyers, determined when usefulness had been fulfilled and sent doctors to do their dirty work. In this world, death wore a white lab coat.

My life's work was selling the concept of usefulness fulfilled, like the admen of old who hooked the world on smoking vile weeds bringing an early demise to those who took the bait. Those hucksters of old were richly rewarded for selling death. I, however, lived as others, toiling in my cell, posting my wicked arguments more directly, to encourage the acceptance of a poison more directly poured into the veins of the no longer useful, or more accurately, no longer useful *enough*. The High Court of the New Way Society had meted out that compromise concerning the barely useful, siding with the cause of death.

So, I at least had a few words left to make me useful, to complete the missive. Having a natural way with words, I had had a long career convincing the less than adequately useful to voluntarily go to the men in the white lab coats, who I now, knowing better, could not call doctors. I had discovered my mind was not my own. And my mind had changed. Long held beliefs I now questioned. And that was dangerous.

My status, as the longest running member of the Oblivion Acceptance Team, allowed me a window in my cell, and the word came two days ago, written in some red substance I assumed was blood, on a leaf tied to the leg of a pigeon.

"Seek the Old Way

The culture of life.

362MW3F 3L 5W"

The culture of life? The Old Way? Of course, there must be an old way if there were a new way. How had I labored so long for this culture of death and not considered this obvious deduction? But what was this old way? This culture of life? Surely, it had been abandoned or snuffed out for its inefficiency. Did it value the lives of the useless, wasting precious resources? How would such a thing make sense and survive? It hadn't. That is how it became the old way. And yet, what of this pigeon? And what was the significance of "362MW3F 3L 5W"?

How could I seek the Old Way? The thought intrigued me. My communications were limited, strictly controlled and monitored. All that came in was that which was necessary for my tasks—documentation on the importance of efficiency and the avoidance of waste and other New Way Society propaganda. Such was the basis for my work. But convincing the useless to accept death went beyond the rational and into the emotional, else a machine could do it as well as I. My usefulness, and thus, my life, depended on this premise.

Why had I not questioned this placing of efficiency over life? Was there something beyond usefulness as a reason to live? What I knew of philosophy spoke of meeting a purpose as what gave value to life. Was this a *New Way* philosophy? Had there been an older philosophy where the value of a life was not derived from its usefulness? Such a thought was contrary to the Creed of the New Way: *We believe that only that which fulfills its purpose has value and its value is measured in efficiency.* But perhaps, there was another creed, an older creed? The note said to seek the Old Way, but how?

Should I report the note? In that way lay danger. I had violated the creed in reading it: *We believe that information is the truth, and the only source of information is the New Way Information System.* Gaining information from an outside source, especially for a member of the Oblivion Acceptance Team, meant an end of one's usefulness. But someone had sent the note and violated the creed, which went beyond ending his usefulness and becoming an agent of *malinformation.* Perhaps this person monitored my work? Had he risked all to reach me? Or could it be some kind of loyalty test? Ink and paper had been outlawed as inefficient in the New Way Society long ago. Most people would struggle to handwrite the characters routinely typed or dictated and taken down as bits of data into the New Way Information System. Would the Ministry of Information have gone so far as to use blood on a leaf delivered by a pigeon to test the

loyalty of an old cog in their machine, approaching the end of its useful life? They needn't go through so much trouble. They could just send the normal end of usefulness documentation which I had expected might come each day for the last five years or so.

But to "seek the old way?" Even to contemplate it was risking diminished usefulness. The only source of information available was the only source of information allowed: the New Way Information System. But surely, searching for the "Old Way" or the "culture of life" would be flagged as suspicious activity by the Ministry of Information. I rarely searched for anything. Curiosity diminished one's usefulness rating. Toiling in silence, meeting your deadlines, these were the keys to survival in the Society of the New Way.

What of this "362MW3F 3L 5W"? Searching for something as cryptic as that would directly inspire a visit from a white-lab-coater with the Happiness of Oblivion shot—that was what they called the poison. The end result was a corpse with a macabre smile, which I had extolled the virtues of in countless missives. But I was not the only one. The Ministry of Information—Oblivion Acceptance Team had many writers. Was this some sort of alternate index to point me to where I should search? The official indexes were machine code. Humans could search on dates or by keywords. Was the sender of this message encoding the index to a document in this strange sequence of characters? Could it be hiding a keyword? Or a date?

I committed the message to memory. I could not afford to be caught with this evidence. The monitors constantly ran and recorded all activity, but only certain activities attracted attention. I was recorded, surely, futzing with the leg of a pigeon, and removing a leaf entangled on it. And glancing several times at the leaf. I walked to the bathroom. I doubted anyone monitored an older man's bathroom. I washed the blood off the leaf and tossed it in the trash. If they found it, they would not find the message. And, if they looked, they would find the leaf. That was important. Disposal of evidence was indicia of guilt.

I made myself useful, a necessity of life, and worked on my next missive on the joys of death. Someone had gone to a lot of trouble to send me a pigeon, an old-school unmonitored method of communication. Was it even intended for me? How did the pigeon know where to go?

...Uncle Jim's lips curled into a smile, I wrote. *Sally glanced at the doctor, who met her eyes gently and took her hand, warmly. Uncle Jim had gone happily into oblivion. He had had a life of supreme usefulness, and now, Sally knew, she would follow in the New Way, where he had led.*

I ended my latest missive and submitted it. It wasn't very good, but I had a deadline to meet, and it hit the essential points. The distraction of this pigeon-delivered note might just send me on the happy way to oblivion. "362M," what was it? Had I forgotten the rest? "362M...W3F." Yes, that was it. "M...W...F." Of course, Month, Week, Friday. It was a date. 362nd month, Week 3, Friday. That's 46 years, ten months. Had the Ministry of Information been at this that long? Had I been at this that long? I started when I was twenty. That would make me sixty-six years old. That was about right. I had lost track of the years in my life of usefulness for the Ministry of Information, separated from the world in my private cell. The tenth month? That would be last month. Now I had something to search for that was less likely to generate inquiries. I checked the date in the system calendar, which I rarely bothered with—a change in behavior that might be noted in the system. Everything was monitored. But it would be less conspicuous than searching for something cryptic. The third week of October, Friday, the 18th.

The missives from the Ministry of Information—
Oblivion Acceptance Division were fictional accounts extolling the virtues of the happiness of oblivion. There were several authors, but the works were never signed. They were missives from the state, not from an individual. I read through the missives for October 18th. There was nothing special about them. Except in one, a curious violation of the line-spacing algorithm. A minor editing glitch. Or was it?

I took a closer look. On the third line, an odd sentence. "Anthony thought that to seek oblivion would be a sin, and he was right. Usefulness must always be the priority."

To suggest that a character would seek oblivion was edgy. Encouraging curiosity. Curiosity decreases usefulness. But that was a word from the note from the pigeon. The fifth word, in the third line. 3L 5W. And there, down the scroll of words, the fifth word in every third line: "seek the old way the culture of life."

I searched the missives for the following days, reading the fifth word in every third line:

"Search and you will find."

"First to die, then the judgment."

"Be transformed by the renewal of your mind."

"The Father gave us the wisdom to understand fully the mystery."

"In Him and through His blood we have been redeemed."

"Seek first the kingdom of dog."

This last one was strange. *The kingdom of dog?* And that word *seek,* again. But there was a familiar ring to a few of these coded messages. Something from long ago, from my childhood. Those days, when people believed in fairytales and went to Churches and listened to priests, before the New Way Human Transformation Programming encoded the

Preconditions for Happiness in my mind. But were they, after all, fairytales? Was this life of usefulness leading to oblivion, the New Way, was it the right way? Was that old way of fairytales and priests, of hope and faith, and, love...when last had I heard these words? When did usefulness become the sole measure of worthiness? Was there an Old Way to seek? Was it to be found in every fifth word of every third line of every thought in my mind? Hidden in some neuro-linguistic puzzle, buried, waiting to be discovered? Who was this *Father?* And who was *He?* And how could *His blood* redeem?

I wrote another missive. In it, on every third line, every fifth word, I embedded a question: *What must I do to follow the old way?*

I submitted the missive and waited. I slept little that night, my mind fighting to regain what might remain of the treasures of the old way, amidst the lines and words of my mind. I dreamt of a stone in front of a cave, rolling away, and woke as a great flash of light from the cave blinded my eyes.

I checked the New Way Information system for the latest missive and found the answer: *Repent and believe in the good news.*

The Old Way, the way of repentance and good news, the old treasures of thought buried from childhood. I recalled the fairytale long rejected, of a man who had risen from the dead. His message: Repent and believe the good news. Thoughts long forgotten. Words long forgotten. *Oh death, where is thy sting?* The New Way Society had sought to remove the sting of death with the Happiness of Oblivion shot. What a mockery! And I had aided them. *The sting of death is sin.* And I had a great weight of sin upon me. In the old way, the way of repentance, there lay the answer—but there was no priest to hear my confession. The New Way, was there someone who could absolve me? Or was the only answer to go gentle into that good night? With the drug-induced smile of the Happiness of Oblivion shot?

The knock had come at my door on this, the third day since the coming of the word on the leg of a pigeon, interrupting my latest missive, which I intentionally left uncompleted. They wouldn't allow me to complete it if they discovered the code. I opened the door and greeted the smiling dealer of death in his white lab coat.

"Yes?" I asked.

He checked his electronic tablet. "Our records indicate that your usefulness rating has descended past the point of viability. As a member of the Oblivion Acceptance Team, I'm sure you know what that means."

"I'm sorry, doctor, I have unfinished business to complete."

"Well, I'm sure you are aware that the Oblivion Acceptance Team likes for its members to set a good example. You are sixty-six years old and have proven useful for six years past the standard expiration date. We have completed all the documents with the legal team. It should only take a minute to administer the Happiness of Oblivion injection."

The man in the lab coat showed me the order on his tablet. It indicated a normal Happiness of Oblivion visit, with no indication that my recent curiosity or work were the cause. That meant, if I completed my missive, it should go through without extra scrutiny. I could appeal and gain a delay, to complete any unfinished business. But to do so, would initiate a review. Would they find the video of my encounter with the pigeon? Would they discover the messages embedded in the missives? Would the review bring discovery of the mysterious source of the Old Way evangelism?

I nodded. "Okay, doctor. It will just take a minute for me to complete the final line of my missive. I'd like to go out completing this one final act of usefulness."

The dealer of death smiled. He would soon have the pleasure of watching me depart this life.

I finished the last line: *Death is the sweetest good-bye and nothing to be feared.* My usefulness at an end, I was ready to face what was coming with a smile. I submitted it. Unknown to the editor and the censors, however, every fifth word of every third line read: *Forgive me Father for I have sinned, good-bye.*

THE GHOST OF HALLOWEEN PAST

AND OTHER CATHOLIC TALES FROM THE EDGE...

A MAN SEEKS ABSOLUTION WITHOUT REMORSE IN A WORLD GONE MAD

THE END OF JUSTICE

Reedsy.com prompt: *Write a story where the laws of time and space begin to dissolve....*

*F*IONA, MY WIFE, LAY dead on the living room floor, and I felt nothing. I glanced at my hand, and the knife, red with her blood, yet not a twinge of conscience. Shouldn't I feel guilt? I reasoned I had committed a grave sin, and knew it to be a sin, and yet, I knew no guilt. I felt greater sorrow for sin when I had stolen a pack of gum from Floyd's Pharmacy when I was nine years old. I had run to confession to the priest, feeling this separation from God that was guilt, seeking absolution. And yet, for this grave sin of murder? Murder of my wife of ten years? Nothing.

I glanced at her, her dead eyes staring at the ceiling. I always loved her eyes. But I could conjure only a vague recollection of love. There was no memory of a sense of it. Only a concept. Something was broken in me. I reasoned I should go to a priest and confess. I went to the bathroom and washed the blood from the knife and from my hands. Glancing to the mirror, I would have to change my clothes. Maybe it would be best to take a shower?

I listened to the radio while I showered. A scientist on the news warned of a problem with the earth moving further from the sun and the moon moving further from the earth. Some unexplainable diminishment in the gravitational force holding the celestial bodies in their place. I thought of the terrestrial body on the floor in the living room. Surely, she would remain in her place.

After I cleaned myself up and dressed, I stepped over her body, a bloody mess, to get to the door. Why had I killed her? I must have wanted to, and there was nothing any longer holding me back from doing whatever I wanted to do. Didn't I used to have something holding me back? A sense of justice? But there was nothing, now. She was just a body I remembered doing things with, but hadn't she been a person? I reasoned that she had been. And I had murdered her. And murder was a sin. And sins, sins you confessed to a priest.

I opened the door and began my walk to the church. Bernie, my neighbor, was getting with a woman on his front lawn. Was she trying to get away from him? We used to go to church together. Would he be heading to confession when he was through with her? I doubted it. I always thought Bernie walked with us to church because he had a crush on Fiona. I often joked about it with her. But I never actually believed he would do anything untoward. He was always pretty uptight and repressed. But he certainly was letting loose now.

I heard a gunshot from across the street, and saw a man, yes, that was Tom Flannegan, fall dead from a bullet shot from a gun held in the hand of his ten-year-old daughter Penny. Tom had been concerned that she was so sullen and introverted. I guess Penny had finally come out of her shell.

I felt no compulsion to interfere with whatever Bernie was doing or to help the shot man. I thought of the people doing these things, Bernie, and Penny. Did they feel guilty? I must not be the only one struggling with lack of conscience, this complete freedom from inhibitions. Would the line for confessions at the church be long? Or was I some kind of weirdo, having reasoned my way into going without the slightest sense of guilt. My intellect sent me where I went, not some grief in my soul for having separated myself from God. Hadn't that grief always been what drove me to confession in the past? But it was just not there.

What would I tell the priest? Would he ask if I were sorry for my sins? I reasoned that I should be. But there was no feeling of sorrow. Must I feel sorrow for my sins to be absolved? Why did I seek absolution? I had some memory that I was supposed to, little more. After all, it would be a sensible thing to do, if it were possible. If there were an afterlife, certainly there would be a great benefit to absolution. But didn't absolution require contrition? And a firm purpose of amendment? I think I could manage a firm purpose of amendment. I had no desire to kill anyone else. I had murdered and gotten no satisfaction or delight from the act. It was just something I did. Why would I find it difficult to resolve not to do it again? But was I contrite? Was I sorry? If I had it to do again, would I? Probably not. But not because it was wrong. Just because, well, what was the point? I had no rational reason for killing her. Was that close enough to contrition? Just to say I wouldn't bother doing it if I had to do it again?

As I approached the church, a squad car raced by with its siren wailing and lights flashing. It screeched to a stop a hundred yards or so past me. Was I concerned about being caught? Facing justice for my crimes? Oddly, no. The policeman got out of his car and gruffly grabbed a middle-aged woman and beat her with a truncheon. I stopped walking and watched. She fell to the ground and appeared unconscious. But the cop kept beating her, likely to death. Was she his wife? Maybe we had something in common. He gave one last heavy blow to her head and glanced at me. I shrugged. He got back into his squad car and drove off.

I reached the large, Gothic church, St. Andrew's. Saint Andrew had been crucified on and X shaped cross. X marks the spot. What an odd thought. I ascended the stairs. A gargoyle had fallen off the facade and lay smashed on the stone steps. Gargoyles were supposed to guard the church from demons. Had the demons vanquished the gargoyle and occupied the church? I chuckled.

I entered through the center portal. The confessionals were at the front of the church on the right side. I blessed myself with holy water and genuflected to—nothing. There was no sense of holiness. Only utter abandonment. The altar was there. The tabernacle was there. But there was no sense of the presence there. The church was lit by candles, dim incandescent lighting, and the colored sunlight shining through the stained glass. I walked toward the front. I recalled that there were some sins that cried out for vengeance, and a couple of dudes engaged in one of them on the steps leading up to the altar. There was a time when I might have been outraged at such a sacrilege. I might have even physically chased them from the church. Or called for help. I chuckled.

The idea of calling for help, calling for the police, struck me as comical. I had witnessed a policeman beating an unarmed woman with a truncheon, among other mayhem, on my walk to the church. The police were not immune from whatever caused this absence of conscience.

I knelt in a pew and waited for the penitent ahead of me to complete his confession. I recalled the act of contrition: *Oh my God, I am heartily sorry for having offended thee.* Was I heartily sorry? I knew I should be. *And I detest all my sins because I dread the loss of heaven and the pains of hell.* Surely, I felt the loss of heaven. Was this hell? This place where I could murder and feel no guilt? It couldn't be. I imagined the pains of hell would be severe, and I felt nothing. *But most of all because I have offended thee, my God, who is all good and deserving of all my love.* I had offended God. But what did it mean to be "all good?" And love? I understood it only as a concept. Putting another's needs before one's own. Sacrifice. I looked to the cross that still hung over the altar. Yes, that was love. But why was my understanding so remote, so conceptual. Like a distant memory. *I firmly resolve, with the help of thy grace, to confess my sins, to do penance, and to amend my life.* Grace? Surely that was what was missing. Like the scientist's report of gravity diminishing, somehow, grace had diminished, and now was nearly wholly absent. Grace was another conceptual thing, not a thing of reality. At least not anymore.

The penitent in the confessional left with a strange, vacant smile on his face. I entered the confessional and knelt. The priest slid the door behind the screen over.

"Bless me Father, for I have sinned. It has been about a month or so since my last confession."

"Go ahead."

"I murdered my wife."

"That's a very serious sin, my son. Why did you do it?"

"That's just it, Father. I don't know. I just figured I could."

The priest sighed audibly. "And do you feel sorry for your sins?"

"I don't feel anything, Father. I know I should feel sorry. I want to feel sorry. But I seem to have lost sense of, well—morality. I have no reaction to evil, or even, a way to judge evil or good. Everything is just action and reaction. I came here, because I know it should be the right thing to do, but it's just conceptually the right thing, not like it should be, with a feeling of guilt. Like I used to feel guilty for sin."

"My son, unfortunately, your experience has become common in these days. It is a sign of the times. Psychologists believe that something has caused an epidemic of psychopathy, but such a thing—there just is no mechanism for it. Science has no explanation for what is happening and relying on science leaves great gaps in understanding. Justice is, uh, dissipating. It's not that you cannot sense justice. Justice, itself, is not there for you to sense. All you will have now is a conceptual idea of right and wrong, so you must use rational judgments to discern what to do. There will be no grace to guide you. You will not be able to sense right and wrong anymore, the way you could in the past."

"Are we in hell, Father? Is that what this separation from grace means?"

"No, my son. It is the final test. Many men of science look at justice as a thing of the mind, but it isn't. It is a dimension of reality built into the fabric of the universe. We sense this dimension through our consciences and the measure in this dimension is guilt or moral satisfaction—the abhorrence of what is evil, the appreciation of what is good and beautiful. But justice, morality, is fully a dimension, just as length or height or width or time. The moral dimension of the universe is becoming what men who did not believe in God thought it to be—just a concept of the mind. This is how it will be until the end. God is unmaking the universe, and part of the fabric of the universe is the dimension of morality. We have only our intellect to guide us, now."

"Can I be absolved if I don't feel sorry? I know I want to be absolved. I know what I did was a sin. I just don't feel guilty."

"Yes, my son. You are as contrite as circumstances allow. Through the ministry of the Church, may God give you pardon and peace. I absolve you of your sins, in the name of the Father, and of the Son and of the Holy Spirit. For your penance, say a rosary for your wife's soul. If you can, before the end comes, give her a Christian burial. That might be difficult, so it is not part of your penance, just something you should do. I would tell you to turn yourself in to the authorities to face justice for your crime, but there is no justice for the authorities to deliver. We are past the time where that is possible."

"Thank you, Father."

"Go in peace."

I exited the confessional. Who knew that justice was a dimension and guilt a measure, much like distance is measured in miles or time measured in hours? As I knelt in a pew to pray my rosary, my penance, a mob of people rushed into the church with axes and started chopping. They chopped statues. They chopped stained glass. And they chopped up the penitent who had confessed before me and who had loitered at the back of the church. One of them ran up the aisle, toward me. The rosary would have to wait. I fled toward the front of the church and exited the nave, slammed the door behind me and wedged it shut. A loud chop at the door, and the blade of an ax popped through.

I scrambled down the stairs. An ancient, heavy wooden door, I pulled it open, shut it behind me, and threw the large wooden bolt to hold it fast. If they tried to chop through, it would take a while. I descended a spiral staircase into the crypt below the church, where countless of our faithful ancestors were laid to rest. I completed my penance and said an extra prayer for the priest, who the ax-wielding mob had likely chopped to pieces.

And I recalled the bible verse that, in the end, the dead in Christ would rise first. And I would have a front-row seat to witness it. What better place was there to be, here at the end of all time, when the world would be remade anew?

THE GHOST OF HALLOWEEN PAST

AND OTHER CATHOLIC TALES FROM THE EDGE...

A MAN DISCOVERS THE EXISTENCE OF GOD ONLY IN HIS ABSENCE

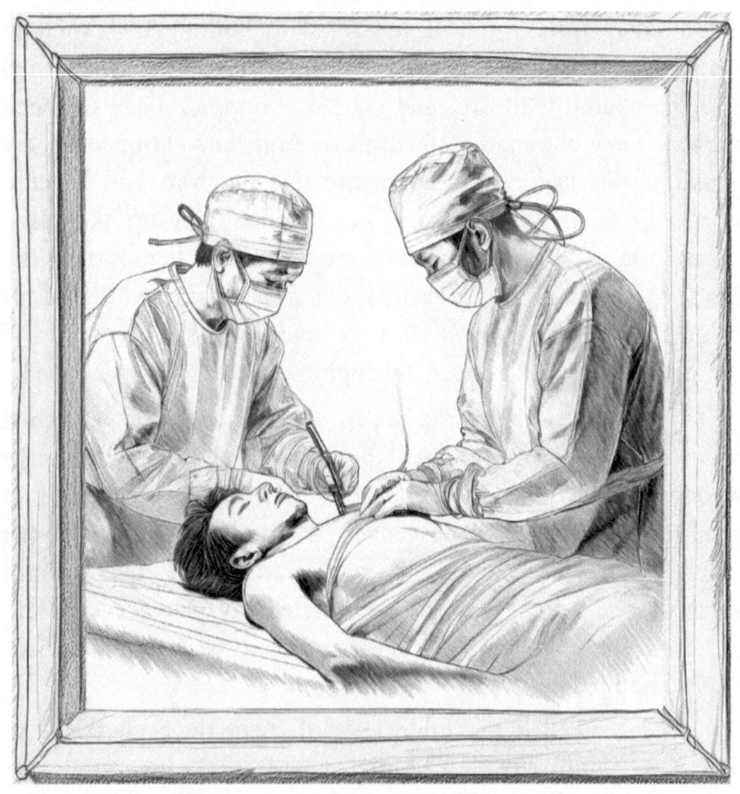

MEMENTO MORI

Reedsy.com prompt: *Start your story with a character in despair....*

So, THIS WAS DEATH. Not far from the nothingness I anticipated—no bliss of heaven, which I had no right to expect, no fires of hell which I, perhaps, deserved. But to be conscious of the nothingness? Who knew? All that was, was no more, except me. I was, in the nothingness. There were no others. There were no other things. Nothing lived in the nothingness, but me. But was I actually alive?

And yet, I remembered all that I used to be. Those I imagined I loved, those I hated, those I ignored, all that was evil, all the evil I had done and what little good—I was alone with my sins, and undeniably knowing with precise clarity the extent and magnitude of each one. Was this some kind of cosmic, eternal time-out?

It was dark. I could see nothing, hear nothing, smell nothing, taste nothing, feel nothing. But there was more missing than what could be sensed in those typical ways. And that was most disturbing. Whatever it was that I had never believed was there, nor wanted to believe was there, was missing.

I knew that which held all things together, the beauty that upheld the universe, created it, nurtured it, loved it—I knew it only now by its absence. And surely, it was gone.

Alone with my thoughts, alone in a way no living thing is ever alone, I was.

Perhaps some men know it while they walk the earth? Those who seek it? Such was the promise, "seek and ye shall find." But I had only sought to deny that which was, and now was not. And here, in whatever this place was, it was not, and its absence was palpable.

"Abandon all hope, ye who enter here"—there was no such sign over some gate to pass through, as Dante suggested. But here, surely, there was no hope. The short few days adding to years of walking in the fallen garden, while there, I had taken for granted all that was important. Had I lived just long enough to know for certain what to miss in this place where nothing was all? So, I might spend eternity remembering that which I should have loved? Was this the cruelty of life? Or was it justice?

Had I lived more boldly, would I have deserved the deepest fires of hell, if such a place existed, and been spared this infernal nothingness? But there were no such flames here. There might be some comfort in knowing I was punished for my crimes, having at least the company of my torturers, hearing the screams of my fellow damned. But, here, would I be alone for all eternity with only the memories of my sins, those things I had done and those things I had not done? I remembered them all. I saw the clear path of righteousness and every step I took from it. I saw every opportunity to believe in that thing that upheld the universe, that thing that grieved each time I stepped away from that path. But that thing was not here, and could never be here. Such, then, was how I imagined creation to be—without a creator. No God to worship. No God to please. No God to forgive. No God to redeem. If this were hell, it was the hell of my own imagining.

There was not even light here, though I imagined a confined space, not some endless nothingness—like a box I could not escape. I had no means to move. No arms, no legs, only this consciousness in this nothingness.

My wife, I remembered my wife, had I ever really loved her? I had turned her, turned her away from faith in things that could not be seen or sensed. Even what I thought of as kindnesses had turned to accusations in my conscience. I had led her to this hell of my creation, this existence without a creator. We sought passion and pleasure in the fleeting gifts of carnality and missed the eternal beauty all around us. The children we prevented, the child we ended before it could be born—they did not fit the lifestyle we chose, the lifestyle *I* chose. I did that to her.

Had I deliberately hurt anyone? Not many, though who does not grab for that which he can have for himself and deny to others? Had I taken more than my share? Had I passed by my neighbors in need?

And what of the insults I hurled at those who believed in that thing that was gone? Had I not instead owed Him my allegiance, my best, all that I was that had come from Him. Oh, how I had scoffed! Who could believe such nonsense? Had He really come as a man to show us how to live? And given His life for our salvation? Why had that all seemed so silly? Such nonsense? But wasn't there something to that crucifix hanging in my mother's house that I now sensed was gone? What was it?

My sister? Yes, she always believed. How I scoffed at her, but I could not shake her from it. Was she now praying for me, casting her kind thoughts into the impenetrable nothingness? She might be, there where there is hope. But here, there was no hope.

What a pedestrian sinner I had been! Denial of God, I suppose that is a big one. And leading others away from faith. Did I know these things were evil? How did I not know? Could I pretend I didn't? But no murder, no adultery, well, once I was married. Fornication, sure. And lies. I lied all the time. Especially to myself. But all my sin was now done. There was no one left to lie to, and no use in lying to myself. Only the truth, the dark, the nothingness, and me. It only got worse with each memory. I had never been what I was meant to be, done what I was meant to do. I had missed it all, deliberately. My God, don't let this be forever! Please, don't leave me here alone with the truth!

I fought against remembering, struggling to be nothing in the nothingness. How could I bear to be the one thing in all the emptiness? Let me be nothing, as well! Annihilation would be a relief, a mercy.

Memento mori, an ancient admonition. Remember death. Remember you are dust and to dust you will return—the words from the Ash Wednesday liturgy when I was a boy. But was I dust? Did I remember my death? How had it come? The doctors, I remembered, the I.V. in my arm, an operation. Yes, they had said it was routine. Very little risk. And then, I was here. I had slipped into death the way those who don't believe in God imagine is the easiest way. The painless way. The way they believe doctors should deliberately grant as a mercy. Was it a mercy? Would a more painful death come with a spiritual cleansing? A scourging, a carrying of a cross, a humbling mocking, would these bring a repentance, and a rescue from this consciousness in the everlasting nothingness? A last gasp for forgiveness from that hidden thing who upheld all that was? Was it better to make coming here, to this eternal darkness easier? I had only questions, no answers. For me, life simply drifted away. The sound of the beeping machines faded to nothing, and the chatter of the doctors and their assistants slipped past hearing and the nothingness began—that nothingness without consciousness inspired by the anesthetics. And then, to awaken here, where I am all that is.

How I missed what had always been there, but I had never acknowledged. I recalled the days of my youth, the promise of salvation, the story of the man who was God who loved sinners, who gave his life for many. The bit of bread on my tongue, I knew now that it had been God, after all. All I had thought a fairy tale to scare children into being good, all I had imagined was a great scam, an inspiration for war and killing, a means of power and coercion. Once that which holds all things together, loves all things, even the evil ones who chose blindness, deafness, defiance—He who makes the rain fall on the good and the bad—once He is gone, and with Him all hope, all that is left is regret and sorrow, all is gone but despair and eternity.

A light, was it a light? The tiniest pinprick of light? But it grew brighter. A faint, long, constant beep. But it grew louder. Muffled voices grew louder.

"That's it. He's gone. Call it."

"Time of death, 2:32 pm."

The snap of a rubber glove. "Well, you can't save them all."

"Wait, doctor. I think I've got a pulse."

THE GHOST OF HALLOWEEN PAST

AND OTHER CATHOLIC TALES FROM THE EDGE...

A POLICE OFFICER LEARNS A LESSON ABOUT OCCULT TATTOOS

THE GOD KILLER

Reedsy.com prompt: *Write a story with a big twist....*

THE MEASURE OF A MAN is made in crisis, and no man knows his measure until that time when he must act, or someone dies.

I knew. And my partner laid dead at my feet. I had frozen. My finger on the trigger of my service revolver, the safety off, waiting for me to act to save my partner, the gun trained on the perp, but I failed to fire. How many times had I made easier shots at the range? But this time, it was for real. And had I but squeezed the trigger, my partner's brains would not be splattered on the wall. My ears rang from the blast of gunfire. I pulled the trigger, finally, repeatedly, emptying the cartridges into the perp, but too late. I closed my eyes for a minute, then engaged the radio and called it in.

"Shots fired. Officer down."

My partner had not hesitated. She had taken two of them down before the one in my sights fired. I had had a clear shot. What held me back? Was it the idea of ending a life? Was it some moral qualm, staying my hand? No, it was fear. I had frozen with fear.

That was months ago. I received a commendation for bravery. What a joke! But no one knew I froze. I had, after all, fired the last bullet and there was no one else to tell the tale. But I knew. I was a coward. And this woman, my partner, who had not hesitated, who had not frozen with fear, was dead because of me. And I, I was decorated.

There was only so much a man could take. Even with the leave of absence and the counseling, I would never be the same. I swore I would not hesitate, again. But who knew? Would I freeze again? Would I get another partner killed? I needed some assurance I would not.

I went to confession. The priest absolved my sins. I did my penance. But this fear still gripped my soul. Did I have what it takes to act when the moment came? Would I freeze again? Would I get someone else killed? The Church did not seem to have the answers.

My new partner was happy to have a highly decorated hero as his partner. If only he knew. At least, it was a man, this time, so I wouldn't have to worry about being shown up by a woman if things got hairy, again.

We busted a couple of meth dealers working out of a tattoo parlor off Old Market Street. Not much of a market on Old Market Street anymore, other than for drugs and tattoos. *Wicked Tats and Potions,* the place was called. I bent one of the perps over the glass display counter and handcuffed him behind his back. Vials of merchandise, presumably the wicked potions, wobbled inside the case. The owner of the place, wearing a top hat and black leather, smiled at us through his facial tattoos and piercings. Hard to imagine this clown was once someone's baby boy, four or five decades ago.

"I know it's called a bust, but try not to break anything, Officers," he said.

I clicked the handcuffs tight, then glanced at the owner. "We will need a statement from you, as well, Mr., uh..."

"Ragnulf, Arne Ragnulf. That translates to Eagle Wolf, I'm told."

Why would I care about the translation of his name? Eagle Wolf? But there was something curious about this man. In fact, his hooked nose did resemble an eagle's beak, and there was an unmistakable tattoo of a dark wolf eating a bright, orange sun on his forearm. More noticeable than any of his physical attributes, the man emanated a penetrating presence, a fearlessness, and a certain hidden, implied ferociousness—as if the spirit of the eagle and wolf vied for control of him. "Well, Mr. Ragnulf, I will take your statement once we have secured the suspects."

Mr. Ragnulf chuckled. "Yes, you will take a statement, but I suspect you will be wanting more from me than that."

The comment took a moment to process. What else would I be wanting from this mook? I glanced around the shop and shook my head. "I doubt very much you have anything I could want. I have no interest in hocus-pocus."

Mr. Ragnulf smiled, knowingly. "The measure of a man is made in crisis. Fear kills more than bullets. A man who takes measures, measures well when the time comes."

I paused and squinted at him. Fear kills more than bullets? "I have no time for riddles. I will return to take your statement."

We secured the detainees in the squad car. I left my partner to watch them and read them their rights. I returned to the shop and took the owner's statement. No, he had nothing to do with the meth traffickers at his shop. Sure, his potions were all legit. Was it believable? Not really, but he spoke with a soft confidence, and stared through me with his eagle-eyes, gray, like a wolf's eyes.

"Okay, Mr. Ragnulf. I think that's it," I said.

"Yes, I see your virgin skin. Have you ever considered taking a mark? We have many customers on the force."

I had noticed my fellow cops, more and more of them, sporting tattoos. But what was the point? Just some ugly thing that would only look worse as you got older—and something that could be used to identify you if you ever got into trouble. I glanced at his sleeve tattoo of the wolf eating the sun. "So, what's the point of the wolf? Trying to mark yourself with a symbol of your name?"

Mr. Ragnulf smiled, then narrowed his eyes. "That is Fenrir, the killer of gods. It is said that whoever wears the mark of Fenrir will fear nothing, not even a god. Or, as you likely believe, the one true God."

I paused. Cops can be superstitious—a constant temptation. When routinely facing danger, it is natural to seek some talisman of protection. My mother had given me a St. Michael's medal. I reached for it under my uniform. It was there, as it had been there when I had failed to act and lost my partner. But St. Michael represented a real entity, an archangel, not some phony pagan god. But had he abandoned me? Was it the way of the poor Carpenter that made me meek and humble, so hesitant to act? Did I need more powerful protection? Was there something to this mumbo jumbo? Could a tattoo make you fearless? A god killer? The image of my dead partner, and her blood, filled my mind.

Mr. Ragnulf nodded. "Yes, a police officer must face many fears. Perhaps, the spirit of Fenrir may help. And the Vegvisir, the Viking Compass, combined, they provide fearlessness and protection. A spiritual sword and shield. Very powerful."

I rolled my eyes. Though intrigued, I wasn't ready to accept this line of bull. It was this guy's business to sell tattoos. There wasn't anything mystical about that. "Superstitious nonsense."

Mr. Ragnulf chuckled. "Perhaps but let me show you the design. Just for fun."

Mr. Ragnulf leafed through a book of designs and pointed to one—an outer circle of runes and an inner circle of witchy-looking symbols pointing out from the center, leading into a wolf's head down the forearm. The thing looked badass, but, well, evil. I couldn't take my eyes off it, though. It seemed to call to me. Could I permanently put this thing onto my body? Would it make me fearless? In the depths of my soul, I knew it was wrong. But, in the depths of my soul, I wanted this thing. I wanted its power. I wanted to be ferocious and fearless, like the wolf—the wolf that killed gods and ate the sun.

I closed my eyes tight and broke away from it. I took a deep breath. "Let me think about it. I've got to get those two clowns down to the station."

Mr. Ragnulf smiled. "Of course. Think about it."

He knew he had me and that I would be back.

So, now I sport a sleeve tattoo of the Viking compass and the wolf, and, it may just be a kind of placebo effect, but I actually think it works. Somehow, my fear is gone. I act without hesitation. My instincts are sharper. If I had it, back on that bad day, would my partner still be alive? That is water under the bridge, now. But even the memory of my fear has faded. Rarely do I imagine that which made her all she was splattered on the wall in that bloody mess. And, when I do, I feel no guilt. That part of me that felt fear, that felt guilt, that questioned my worth, is gone. And good riddance.

There is a beauty to the thing, this mark now permanently part of my body. I find myself in idol moments looking at it, caressing the ink lines of the wolf's fur. Do I feel the spirit of the wolf in my soul? Sometimes, it feels this way.

My phone rings. It's Father Andrew.

"Hey Father Andrew. How can I help you?"

"Tony? We haven't seen you in church for a while. I was just calling to see if you are okay?"

A wave of irritation washes over my soul. I rub my arm over the tattoo. "Yeah, Father, I haven't felt much like praying lately. Been busy with work."

"Well, you know the spirit needs nourishment, just like the body. Why don't you stop in for Holy Hour tonight at eight? It might do your soul some good."

"My soul is just fine, Father!" I respond, angrily, turning off the phone. "Your pathetic carpenter can't help me."

I spare the priest hearing this blasphemy. Am I now referring to my Lord and Savior as a pathetic carpenter? But even asking this question fills me with rage. I rip the St. Michael medal off of its chain and throw it across the room. I rub my arm and take a moment to calm down. I will not be able to make Holy Hour tonight, anyway. I've got to leave now for patrol duty.

We make the usual rounds in our squad car. A slow night. A call comes in. Some woman reporting a prowler. My partner answers dispatch and confirms the call. We arrive at the address, exit our squad car, and inspect the yard with our flashlights. No one around. A car is parked in the driveway, with a smashed passenger window. Was it the work of the prowler? No one here now, though.

I knock on the door of the residence. "Sheriff's office. You called about a prowler?"

No one answers. I knock again. "Sheriff's office. You called about a prowler?"

I wait for a response. The door opens. A middle-aged African American woman in a bathrobe. Need to take care, racial sensitivity. She's futzing with her phone.

"My God, my God," she says, "you need help."

"I need help? Ma'am, you called us for help. We checked for a prowler. We couldn't find anybody." I glance toward my partner. Something is off about this woman.

"My God, my God, you need help. I called because of a prowler."

Each time she says *my God*, it irritates me more and more. We are here to help. Why is she calling for God? "Yes, ma'am. We checked. We didn't see anybody. Are you okay?"

"Me? I'm okay. I've taken my meds. I'm okay. You, you need help?"

I glance at my partner, then back toward the woman. "Would you like us to check the inside of the house?"

"My God, my God, can I help you?" The woman backs off into the house, inviting us in.

The house is a mess—dirty clothes lying around, books and papers scattered on the table, a tea kettle heating on the stove. We need to get some info for our report and see if this woman is okay.

My partner and I step into the house.

"Could you hand me that bible?" she asks, motioning to a book on the table.

I reach for the book, but my arm stops. I can't seem to do it. "Can we get your name for our report, ma'am?"

"Musser, Elise Musser, is my name. I need help."

She fumbles with the phone and calls the sheriff's office. "I need help. Yes, they are here. I need help. Please stay on the line. Just wait a minute."

Something is really off about this woman. "Ma'am, do you have any ID?"

She fumbles in her purse. I watch carefully. She might draw a weapon.

"My God, my God. You need help."

"We're here to help you, ma'am."

"Help me?" She chuckles. "I rebuke you in the name of Jesus."

I draw my weapon and point it at her. "You better not! I'll shoot you in the face if you do!"

I cannot believe the words coming from my mouth. What is happening?

My partner draws his weapon, as well, following my lead. "Slowly, take your hands out of the purse!"

Did he think I saw a weapon in her purse?

"I rebuke you in the name of Jesus," she repeats.

I stare down the gun sights at her. She pulls her hand swiftly from her purse. The wolf tattoo descends my arm and bites the trigger.

Bang!

The shot blows through her skull. Her brains, like my former partner's, splatter on the wall. No hesitation, no fear. Not even of God. As promised.

"Holy crap!" I hear my partner's voice.

And in her hand? A weapon: a bottle of holy water. No way I can avoid going down for this one. I glance at the tattoo on my forearm. The wolf seems to smile. Fenrir: the killer of gods.

THE GHOST OF HALLOWEEN PAST

AND OTHER CATHOLIC TALES FROM *THE EDGE*...

THE MEASURE OF A MAN...

THE GHOST OF HALLOWEEN PAST
AND OTHER CATHOLIC TALES FROM THE EDGE...

A PRIEST ENGAGES IN A BATTLE OF WITS WITH THE DEVIL.

THE DEVIL SMOKES MARLTONS

Reedsy.com prompt: *Center your story around someone facing their biggest fear or enemy....*

*T*HE DEVIL SMOKES MARLTONS. I know because he offered me one.

"Cigarette?" A smile curled the corners of his lips—confident, almost smug. He wore an Armani suit, not some crazy red getup. He carried no pitchfork, though I would not be surprised if his tongue were forked.

Now, it is never wise to converse with an ancient being who knew most all that ever happened, was created with super intelligence beyond the imagining of man, and who detested you and every creature like you since the very idea of your race came into the mind of God. Long ago, an ancestor of mine had made that mistake and broke the world. I ignored him and returned to reading my book.

"Of course not," he said with a chuckle, pocketing his smokes. "It's not an apple, you know. It's not a sin to smoke."

No, it wasn't a sin. It was just a stupid thing to do. That didn't stop me from trying it once. But it only took once. I recalled explaining that to a friend who smoked—the violent coughing and hacking from a single puff. He had had the same reaction but claimed the virtue of persistence had led him to the joys of nicotine addiction. I focused on this memory, avoiding interacting with the fallen angel, amidst the curling smoke of his cancer stick.

"You can't avoid me forever, you know. Come on! Give the devil his due"

I chuckled, and that was a mistake. I refocused on my reading.

"Ah, a reaction. A little respect." He bowed and swung his arm in a gesture of mockery, the cigarette between his fingers.

I tightened my lips and glanced down at my book. I read aloud, "And I saw an angel coming down from heaven, having the key to the bottomless pit and a great chain in his hand."

"Skipping ahead, I see. We're not quite there yet. Go back a little: 'And it was given to him to make war with the saints and to overcome them.' I like that part better."

I continued reading. "And he laid hold of the dragon, the old serpent, which is the devil and Satan, and bound him for a thousand years."

"And all that dwell upon the earth adored him..."

He dared not finish the rest of the verse, *whose names were not written in the book of life of the Lamb which was slain from the beginning of the world.* Quite an exception. He deliberately left that out. He was goading me to finish it, to correct him, to engage with him.

"St. Michael the archangel," I began the prayer composed by Blessed Pope Leo XIII.

"Oh, not him, again."

"Defend us in battle. Be our protection against the wickedness and snares of the devil."

He feigned astonishment. "Wickedness? Oh really."

"May God rebuke him, we humbly pray..."

"Are you really so humble?"

"And do thou, oh prince of the heavenly host..."

"Prince? Have you seen how they depict him? More like princess.'

"By the power of God, thrust into hell Satan..."

"Enough!" he shouted. His eyes lit with flame. "That time is not now!"

My book, the Holy Bible, flew from my hands across the room. I walked over and picked it up, taking no notice of him. That attack on his pride seemed to enrage him, but it was all show. The devil is a loser, and he knows he is a loser. He knows the end of the story. His time is short, but his time at the top has just begun—his war with the saints, whom he will overcome.

I finished my prayer. "Thrust into hell Satan and all the evil spirits who prowl about the world seeking the ruin of souls."

Like a snake, slithering to find a better angle of attack, he calmed himself and took a new approach. He chuckled again. "Well, look at that. No St. Michael thrusting anyone into hell. Have you evidence that your prayers have any effect?"

Questions, questions, questions! How they begged for answers. But that was the trap. You could not out-argue the Father of Lies, the King of Lawyers. It was like playing chess against a master. Once you began to play, you began to lose. I knew from experience. That game, I could not win.

"You pray all the time. How many Masses? How many rosaries? How many novenas? And what has it gotten you? Your family? Your brothers and sisters? Your nieces and nephews? Which of them do you believe are not under my sway?"

I opened my bible, once more, and read aloud, just two verses from his last incomplete quote. "He that shall lead into captivity shall go into captivity: he that shall kill by the sword must be killed by the sword. Here is the patience and the faith of the saints."

"*Patience and faith?* Wait and hope, while those you love are lost. What of your bishop? He, too, is mine. And your pope. *Patience and faith?* How will it save them?"

More questions, more goading. Patience and faith my only defense. I found the place in the bible where I had left off and read on. "And he cast him into the bottomless pit and shut him up and set a seal upon him, that he should no more seduce the nations till the thousand years be finished."

The devil laughed, flinging the book from my hands, again. "Once more, skipping ahead, I see. Will you wait and hope through it all? Or will you act to save those you love? Has love so little meaning for you?"

The door to my cell opened. An orderly stepped in. "Father Michael? If you insist on throwing your bible at the wall, we will have to take it from you."

"I'm sorry, lad, you know I am not well. Have patience with me."

The orderly picked up the bible and set it on my nightstand. "It's time for your appointment with Dr. Simmons. Please come with me."

"Oh, what happened to Dr. Schmidt? I had come to enjoy our talks."

The orderly shuffled his feet. "Dr. Schmidt is no longer with us. Dr. Simmons has taken over his cases."

Psychiatrists could not possibly help my condition, but it did no good to protest. We walked down a long corridor and turned left into Dr. Simmons' office. Dr. Simmons glanced up from reading a file on his desk. He was a young man, likely not yet thirty—the age of arrogance for many, when confidence exceeds ability.

"Ah, yes, Father Michael. Please have a seat."

I took a seat across the desk from him. "It's nice to meet you, Dr. Simmons. But I had been looking forward to seeing Dr. Schmidt."

The devil's lips curled into a sinister smile. "Ah, yes, Dr. Schmidt. He never would have let us out, you know."

As if there was an *us*.

"Dr. Schmidt is no longer with us," Dr. Simmons said.

"Oh, I hope he is okay?" I asked.

"Nothing for you to worry about. Just an employment dispute. He had recommended some unorthodox therapies that did not fit with our protocols."

The devil chuckled. "He means, Dr. Schmidt recommended an exorcist be consulted. Now, that would never do. That's the kind of thing that got us into this mess."

I sighed.

Dr. Simmons glanced at my file. "So, it says here that you see the devil. Is that right?"

The devil mocked me now, appearing with the red suit, horns and pitchfork. "Go ahead, Father Michael. Tell him you see me."

I rolled my eyes. "I'm sure you can rely on Father Schmidt's notes. Must I really repeat it all, again."

Dr. Simmons glared at me. "Father Michael, if you won't be candid with me, I can't help you."

I shook my head. "You cannot help me with psychotherapy, because I don't have a psychological condition."

"Come now, Father! Are you saying you actually believe that you see the devil? The devil isn't real."

"Well, now, that's a matter of faith, isn't it doctor? Don't I have a right to believe what my religion teaches?"

"You may believe, Father, but to see things that aren't there, that is a different matter."

"And how do you know he isn't there? How do you know he isn't there right now, all in red, horns on his head, and waiving a pitchfork."

And of course, he was.

The devil snickered. "Good luck getting him to believe that one."

The doctor shook his head. "Your case is indeed serious..."

"Yes, doctor," I interrupted. "It is serious. Please allow me to consult an exorcist. You can observe the whole thing."

The devil laughed. "Sure, I'll put on a grand show for him."

The doctor tilted his head. "You're a priest. Why don't you just say your mumbo-jumbo and banish him, or whatever you do."

I leaned back in my chair. "It's gone too far for that. I have walked in his darkness. I allowed him in. I made a mistake."

The devil raised his eyebrows. "Will you tell it to the doctor? What you did? He cannot absolve you."

"Father Michael, the circumstances of your involuntary commitment are quite serious. A fellow priest and a young girl are dead. You are lucky not to be on death row."

I put my head in my hands. I didn't want to review the details. I had explained it all to Dr. Schmidt and it had taken a year to get him even to consider consulting an exorcist. *Wait and hope. Patience and faith.* "I had a good lawyer."

"The best!" the devil interjected, unheard by the good doctor.

"It says here you represented yourself." Dr. Simmons glanced up over the file and met my eyes.

I closed my eyes a moment. How could a make a psychiatrist understand? "Have you ever heard of the devil's advocate?"

"Yes, wasn't that part of the process for determining sainthood?" Dr. Simmons asked.

"Well," I chose my words carefully, "I have found, from experience, that the devil needs no advocate. He is a most accomplished barrister. I have little memory of what happened at my trial."

The doctor raised his eyebrows. "So, you are saying that you believe the devil represented you and that is how you managed to avoid conviction?"

"Jolly good of you to give me the credit," the devil said.

"I was acquitted by reason of insanity. I am a priest, not a lawyer. I have no memory of how he did it. I only know he can be very persuasive. He wants me here for now, not on death row. And he doesn't want me seeing an exorcist."

"In my opinion, Father Michael, consulting an exorcist would only feed your delusion." The doctor met my eyes and his gaze did not waver.

"What do you know?" the devil butt in again, "A man of conviction. What do you bet I can persuade him to let us out? It would be a great victory for science in his eyes."

I closed my eyes and tried to calm myself. I would never take that bet. "It is better for you, and for the world, that I am here, and he is with me."

"You may have gotten yourself acquitted of the charges, but you will remain committed here, unless we determine you are better. I don't think it likely you will ever get out," the doctor said, "if you don't trust me. Tell me what happened."

"You see!" said the devil, "He wants to help us. I'm sure I can get him to let us out."

"You won't believe me," I said, "and you will use my account as evidence of psychosis. Will that really help my case? It would be dangerous to leave without consulting an exorcist, anyway. Here, he has little influence. Especially because I have gotten used to ignoring him."

"So, you have these visions, but you know they are not real, so you ignore them?"

"No, I ignore him, because I know he is real."

The devil was back in his Armani suit. He took a puff on his cigarette. "If you play ball with this guy, he will let us out of here."

"But if he is real," the doctor said, "why can't you demand that he leave?"

"Do you think I haven't tried that? I have gone through the entire exorcism rite, at least as much as I can remember. I've done all I can with prayer and fasting. I've gotten him this far out, that I control myself. But he's always itching, prodding, cajoling for a way back in. If I interact with him, I open a door that must stay shut. I need the assistance of an exorcist with faculties from the bishop to go further."

"Ah, the bishop," the devil said, "he'll never grant faculties. He's one of my useful idiots. He doesn't believe I exist. Our only chance is to work with this guy. Just deny I exist. He'll let us out, if he thinks you're better."

"So, you know your mumbo-jumbo doesn't work," the doctor said. "Let us try to help you with psychotherapy. I'm sure we can help. You just need to stop feeding this delusion."

"You see!" said the devil. "He is ready to help us. To get us out of this prison! Just go along with him, and he'll let us out."

"It would be too dangerous to let us out!" I blurted.

"Us, who is us?" the doctor asked.

"Tell him," the devil said. "Then, he can think he is helping us, and get us out. Tell him about us."

"No, I meant *me*. It would be dangerous to let *me* out," I stammered.

"Are there more than one of you?" the doctor asked.

The devil leaned forward, with his hands on the desk across from me. "Yes, say yes. He will think he can cure us. Then, we will be on our way."

"No, doctor, there is one of me and one of him. There is no us."

"Oh, yes, there is an us. We are in this together. I got us off of the charges. Now, you get us out of here!" The devil's voice crescendoed to a thunderclap in my head, as he pounded the desk with his hand.

I covered my ears. "There is no *us!*" I shouted, glaring at the devil in exasperation.

"There is now," The devil replied.

My soul veiled itself behind his possession. I had slipped up again. With the girl, it had been the thought of helping others, my family. To walk through the darkness to save their souls. I had come to with the bloody crucifix in my hand, having beaten my fellow priest and the girl to death. I don't know what the devil said to Dr. Simmons through me, but I became aware of him. Doctor Simmons, not believing the devil existed, had no defenses in prayer to turn to. What had been the reason for his consent? What promises? What pomp and empty show? I would never know. But now, not a vision, but in Dr. Simmons, I saw him, puffing a Marlton cigarette.

"Thanks, for the ride, priest. I have much to do before the angel comes with the chain to bind me."

THE END?

HERE ENDS OUR COLLECTION of Catholic tales from the edge, but there are always more...

If you enjoyed this work, please take a few moments to write a brief review–just a few words to help others know what you liked about it. Every word is greatly appreciated.

Check out EdgyCatholic.com, where there is always more free stuff...

GHOST OF HALLOWEEN PAST

AND OTHER CATHOLIC TALES FROM THE EDGE...

A FEW WORDS ABOUT THE AUTHOR

ABOUT THE AUTHOR

JOSEPH CILLO, JR. writes edgy Catholic fiction in a variety of genres. Whether it's a supernatural thriller like his graphic novel, Blind Prophet or a comedy like the 2019 Illumination Book Award Bronze Medal winner, Merry Friggin' Christmas: An Edgy Christmas Comedy, his work features unexpected plot twists, unique characters, and the highest of stakes.

The added dimension of the supernatural infuses his work with stakes that go beyond life and death, and into the eternal. There is a basic, Catholic moral viewpoint behind his work that gives a solid foundation to what might otherwise be seen as purely fantastical. The reading experience can at times be unnerving, as the reader is drawn to consider whether the mystical nature of his tales is nearer to reality than the plainly material experiences of life. The eternal consequences of choices made by characters and spiritual dimensions of actions made clearly visible are mind-bending and thought-provoking.

Joseph Cillo, Jr. classifies his writing as Edgy Catholic Fiction. Edgy Catholic Fiction is generally written for adult audiences, at minimum teens and up. The grouping crosses genres and includes a perspective that is generally consistent with the teachings of the Catholic Church, which may include rather dramatic supernatural elements, as in the horror movie, The Exorcist, or other less dramatic religious elements, which could be as simple as characters relying on prayer. The religious elements may not be overt and could well lie only in the author's general perspective or a character's perspective that there is a God, and a moral, immutable foundation to the universe.

For more information, please check out www. edgycatholic.com

Examples of Edgy Catholic literature lie strewn throughout genres which no one has grouped together. Literary masters such as Graham Greene, Flannery O'Connor, J.R.R. Tolkien, and even, C.S. Lewis, who though not Catholic, was consistent with the Catholic perspective in his fiction, wrote works that fall into the Edgy Catholic domain. Dean Koontz, whose supernatural and suspense thrillers are written from a Catholic perspective and are quite edgy, is a more contemporary example of an Edgy Catholic author.

Joseph Cillo, Jr. is the fourth of seven children, born within a year of his older sister in a most unplanned and yet welcome way. Having the great blessings of a loving family, however, did not prevent his drift into a sort of foolhardy extended adolescence for many years, broken only by suffering and illness, in a rather miraculous fashion. He now lives a life of quiet prayer and diligent work.

THE GHOST OF HALLOWEEN PAST

AND OTHER CATHOLIC TALES FROM THE EDGE...

MEMENTO MORI

ALSO BY JOSEPH CILLO JR.

Merry Friggin' Christmas: An Edgy Christmas Comedy

When the Wood Is Dry: An Edgy Catholic Thriller

Elektra Voltare: Blessed with Awful

Elektra Voltare: Eve of the Memes

Elektra Voltare: Instrument of God

BLIND PROPHET COMIC BOOKS

Episode 1: A Prophet Is Born

Episode 2: Spiritual Warfare

Episode 3: The Prophet Goes to Washington

Episode 4: The Great Demon of Pride

Part I (Includes Episodes 1 thru 4)

Get Blind Prophet, Episode 1: A Prophet Is Born for FREE!

For details, please visit: www.edgycatholic.com

www.ingramcontent.com/pod-product-compliance
Lightning Source LLC
Chambersburg PA
CBHW031254210726
48287CB00003B/1037